I0548312

LUCIFINA: THE BELLE OF HELL

Licia Flynn
ISBN: 978-1-7322777-5-5

Klar Marketing Communications

Special thanks to my editor, Nina Denison.

CONTENTS

CHARACTER LIST

*Critical characters are bolded

Lucifina (Fina) – Main character; Satan's twin sister
Beelzebub – Fina's archnemesis; Satan's right-hand man; frequently delivers messages to Fina
Raphael – Angel sent by God to persuade Fina to return to Heaven
Mom (Marie) – Blonde, blue-eyed mother of Fina
Herman – Kitty's ex-boyfriend; house-guest for the summer
Aaron Walker – Recurring character in Flynn's novels (*Firm Resolve* and *Firm Denial*)
Selina – Fina's best friend; a beautiful Eurasian model and pop singer
Evelina – Selina's older sister; a soap opera star
Jess – Male model and notorious player; friend of Fina
Khun Jin – Fina's current modeling agent
Blackie the Cat – Fina's childhood pet; Blackie wears a tuxedo and allegedly prevented a neighbor, Khun Yao, from choking to death
Khun Yao – Neighbor
Satan – Fina's twin brother who rarely appears be-

cause he's too busy running Hell.

Khun Jai – Family housekeeper

Belial – A demon in Hell; the object of Fina's long infatuation

Apple – Neighbor

Dad – Fina's father

Kitty – Fina's sister; Herman's ex-girlfriend

Terry – Fina's classmate

Carly – Fina's classmate

Jack – Fina's personal assistant

Khun Choke – Fitness instructor at Clark Hatch

Troy Walker – Father of Aaron

Chad – Male model and thorn in Fina's side

Ms. Tracy – Bible teacher

Roxanne Barger – Tom Barger's daughter

Tom Barger – Family friend of Mom (Marie)

Khun B – Fina's modeling agent while she was 14-18

Alice – Modeling agent; Fina's booker in Singapore

Janet – Mom's friend

Lydia – Mom's friend

Tania – Daughter of Mom's friend

Tony – Male model

PART 1: THE RISE AND FALL

CHAPTER 1: BACKGROUND – THE WAR IN HEAVEN

Before the revolution, many escaped. Most were bad.

I envy victims who despise their perpetrators. Hatred is a powerful, motivating force. It mobilizes troops. Whereas guilt—well, it can be debilitating.

My name is Lucifina. Billions of years ago, I lived in Heaven with my twin brother, Satan.

Satan is the most charming and charismatic leader ever to exist. But he frequently challenged God.

Thus, my brother used his rhetorical skills to organize his followers: Mammon, Beelzebub, Belial, and Moloch.

A fierce, large-scale war in Heaven ensued.

The revolution was long and bloody. We fought artfully through a systematic strategy known as "quick, quick, slow."

Unfortunately, we were no match for Gabriel and the Son of God. These two fought boldly against Satan and his rebel angels.

In the end, our ragtag army was ousted from Heaven. We took refuge in Hell and set up our capital city of Pandemonium.

Some of us preferred exile. After all, we were finally free.

However, my brother isn't one to give up easily. His valiant efforts to destroy Earth have consistently failed.

Thus, I was repeatedly sent to Earth—always as an attractive woman. I was Hell's secret weapon. My mission: to recruit and ultimately control leaders throughout the world.

So much has been written about Satan. Rarely, if ever, does anyone discuss his twin sister. Now it's my turn. Everyone needs to know about Lucifina.

This is my story. If you seek a tale about a virtuous heroine who consistently does the right thing, might I recommend any other book?

CHAPTER 2: INFANCY

On a warm summer's day, my soul was reborn. This time, I was Fina. Like any demon, I put my mother through unspeakable agony. Mom was sick for nine months, throwing up anything she ate. When she finally went into labor, I made sure it was for over forty-eight hours. In a different century, she would have died. But the doctors cut her open and salvaged me.

When my parents first saw me, they exclaimed, "Our little angel!" Satan had designed the perfect disguise. I now possessed the body of an ethereal girl. No one suspected my genuine character because people always believe what they want. Through divine inspiration, my parents chose the name Fina.

Rarely was I treated like a child. It's as if everyone knew I was an old soul—one who had scourged the universe since the beginning of time. I had consciousness by two and listened to my parents like a therapist. Everyone had so much to say. I didn't mind because I was inquisitive. Unfortunately, there are grave dangers in being a good listener and possessing a strong memory. You're often privy to things you'd rather not know. And it's hard to trust people when you've ascertained inconsistencies in their stories.

Details of my former lives lingered, but faded with the succession of each human life. During infancy, I heard the voices of mature women shouting cautionary words such as, "darling, oh, do be careful," "please beware," or "this has happened before."

During high tea, I liked perching on a red velvet chair where I could nibble scones and watch the sparrows through the window. Mom expressed her anxiety with the world. I nodded sympathetically but questioned her expectations. After all, life is chaos.

Sometimes, Mother confided in me about family squabbles. I would tilt my head to the side while thinking, *Mother, my father's people are hardly known for their sensitivity to the fairer gender. I can't imagine they'll ever change.*

Meanwhile, Dad ranted and raved about his family and business problems. He was a complicated individual who possessed the wisdom of an ancient tribe. His ancestors could trace their roots back to the beginning of civilization when writing began.

My parents were cruel because they dressed

me in frilly dresses trimmed with lace and sent me to a formidable prison where children milled about. Such an institution seemed superfluous. After all, I was Lucifina, a billion-year-old demon who knew everything. I didn't need school. Unfortunately, over time the memories of my past were replaced with current life experiences.

My life as a demon had been relatively sheltered. Satan ran Hell with an ironclad fist whereby all demons were relegated to specialized roles. It was rare that anyone could see the big picture. Affecting extreme naivete and even ineptitude is a survival tactic adopted by some living in authoritarian climates. My tactics worked because my supervisors dropped their guard, and I became privy to confidential secrets.

CHAPTER 3: TEEN YEARS — BANGKOK, THAILAND

I sat on a stool in the changing room of a cold studio. The crew had taken a break to fix the lights.

"Lucifina, what the Hell are you doing?" Satan demanded.

I clutched my cell phone. "Focusing on my modeling career."

"You're supposed to be destroying Earth."

"Oh, yeah, well…"

"Well, what?"

"There's not much for me to do."

"Jesus, you're worse than Belphegor," my brother snapped.

"And you're worse than God!"

"Of course, I'm Satan."

"Earth is destroying itself. There's very little

for me to do," I said tersely while rifling through *Cosmo*. I was bored, so I tossed the magazine aside and began filing my nails.

"I gave you the easiest task, yet you can't handle it."

"My mission to recruit the leader of Russia is going well."

"Lucifina, you sent the guy 101 emails."

"Yes, that last one was just in case he didn't get the first hundred."

"Are you insane?"

"Well, insanity runs in our family."

"How the Hell are you my twin?"

"Ah, well, during pregnancy, very often—" I babbled nervously.

"Please shut up," Satan ordered.

"Give me another chance," I begged.

"Not this time."

"Did you at least read my messages to Putin?"

Satan exhaled impatiently. "You wrote: *Dear Vlad, I'm so glad you're in charge because Russia is so large.*"

I beamed. "Poetic, isn't it?"

"This is garbage."

"I'll try again."

"You're done."

I sprung off the stool onto my feet. The cement was freezing. "What?"

"You're off this case."

I gripped the phone tightly and dug my sharpened nails into my palms. "Do I get a new one?"

"Nope."

I gasped. "Why?"

"Lucifina, all you do is waste time."

"Satan, I'm playing the long game." I was now rapidly pacing the room.

"No, you're stalling."

"I'm not."

"We've all had it with you."

I froze, but tilted my head. "We?"

"Don't play innocent."

I crossed my arms as if a blade had pierced through the hollow of my chest. I imagined the other demons: Beelzebub, Moloch, Belial, and Belphegor, sitting around the board room in Hell, evaluating my performance.

Despite my best efforts, I could never meet any of their expectations, especially not Satan's. I was constantly criticized for "being full of feeling," as Beelzebub had snidely put it. The other demons were consistently cold and calculating. Fire burned through my veins, which I fought to suppress. But even when I bit my tongue, my cheeks still blushed.

I swallowed hard. "What does this mean?"

"You're out."

"But without Hell's support, I'll have no power," I stammered while my hands trembled.

"Yep," Satan replied.

"I'll become human."

"You already are."

"Don't leave," I begged.

"Unless you can prove your value to Hell, you can't ever return," Satan snapped. He abruptly ended the call before I could respond.

I listened to the lonely sound of the dial tone and shivered.

How would I survive on Earth alone? What would I do without Hell's support?

A cold breeze penetrated my bones, which felt unusual. My body temperature was typically overheated.

The argument with Satan had overwhelmed me. I was still shaking. So, I sat down on a stool and gazed at my reflection in a mirror adorned with light bulbs.

Was it my imagination? My oval face was looking fuller. My fair complexion looked dryer, my hair less black, and my typically plump lips—defined by a cupid's bow—thinner.

What was happening? I touched my high cheekbones and my nose's arch to make sure they remained. I blinked rapidly and could see red lines in the whites of my brown, almond-shaped eyes. Satan's threats were coming true. I was losing my power.

The makeup artists had run off to get iced-coffee drinks. I stared at the cluttered trays of makeup. Then I pulled out my cell phone again and called Hell's main office.

The dial tone beeped slowly. Finally, Demon Dim Bulb answered, "Hey, what's up? Welcome to Hell."

"Dim Bulb, I need to speak to Satan, please."

"I'm sorry Ma'am, please hold on the line."

"Dim Bulb, wait. It's me, Lucifina."

"Who?"

"Oh, never mind," I wailed and switched off the phone.

I heard someone barking, "Fina, Fina? Where's the talent?"

"Coming," I shouted while bouncing up and running into the studio.

The photographer analyzed me approvingly. He then directed me to sit in an elegant chair. It looked like something from the Louvre. I was wearing a Chanel suit, and my hair was wavy from hours spent in hot rollers.

I glanced around, wondering why the makeup artist and hairstylist hadn't returned. I was the only female in the room. The modeling industry in Bangkok was very male, but predominantly gay.

I began modeling at fourteen. Now, three years later, I was a veteran, having starred in countless cosmetics commercials, music videos, and print advertisements.

I had been the "talk of the town," as my

booker teased. Or the "flavor of the month," as Mom joked.

While sitting on the velvet chair, I stared into the bright lights and smiled.

"I need a more sensual look," the photographer stated.

I blinked rapidly. Focusing was a struggle. *Was it my tiff with Satan? Goodness gracious, I shouldn't have answered his call during a shoot.*

I smiled again, perhaps too sweetly.

The photographer shook his head impatiently while the crew groaned. They were anxious to finish so they could return home.

"That's not sexy. You're like a little girl."

I sighed and thought: *That's because I am a girl.* But no one cared.

The photographer lowered his chin, knelt to the ground, and peered up at me. He teased with a warm smile, "Okay, darling, pretend all the men here are naked."

Good God, I thought and immediately crossed my legs and arms. My face tensed.

"No, no! That's *not* the look I want."

I hugged myself more tightly, blinked rapidly, and clenched my jaw.

The photographer looked down at the ground. He then slowly raised his head and suggested, "Pretend you're the supermodel of the world."

Instantly, I dropped my chin, opened my

arms, tilted my head to the side, and stared into the camera with renewed confidence.

"Hey, that's it." the photographer shouted. "Keep that expression."

I began rapidly shifting angles and altering poses. In the background, I heard pleasant sighs and *click, click, click.*

"Okay, I think we've got it. That's a wrap."

The crew began cheering. The shoot was complete.

***

The room cleared within seconds, and I was all alone. The crew packed their cameras, lighting, and equipment swiftly. Meanwhile, it took me forever to remove my bobby pins and layers of makeup.

After changing, I departed the empty studio and worked my way down dark cement hallways. The smell of paint made me nauseous. It was a reminder that I hadn't eaten the entire day. I scurried quickly to get out of the building, where I encountered crowds rushing home from work.

In the middle of a congested intersection, I observed temples, hawkers, and crowds. The Thai word for Bangkok is *Krung Tep,* which means the "City of Angels." This intoxicating city was a unique blend of several Asian cultures with a heavy Western influence. This Kingdom was renowned for her artful diplomacy because she avoided colonialization without resorting to violence. Unfortunately, hints of covert operations lingered, suggesting that things are rarely what they seem. Within any prescribed culture, the worst of human nature is most repressed and therefore eager to ignite. Vibrant colors and the din of loud noises enhanced Bangkok's bustling energy.

After managing to catch a taxi and endure hours of traffic, I reached a townhouse nestled at the end of a cul-de-sac. I loved its iron gate, flowing trees, and plants that created a jungle-like atmosphere. Our home reminded me of a nineteenth-century Caribbean painting.

While leaping onto the porch sheltered by white pillars, I realized I was walking into an empty house. Mom was still at work, Dad was away, and my sister was at her friend Trixie's.

I bounced upstairs to my bedroom beset with a single bed covered by a white bedspread and lacy pillows. Adjacent was a vanity filled with jewelry boxes and perfume bottles. To my left sat a white rattan peacock chair next to a white screen.

On the wall was a picture of Vivien Leigh from the film *Waterloo Bridge.* A desk sat at the other side of the room opposite dresser drawers. Shelves hung on the walls, which contained Victorian-era poetry, Degas prints, and statutes of ballerinas.

I pulled out my phone and began calling Hell

again, but the line was disconnected. I couldn't even reach Dim Bulb. Evidently, Satan's threat was genuine. I had indeed lost my demon powers and becoming human was genuine.

CHAPTER 4: THE NEXT DAY

Kitty and I stood quietly, waiting for the bus. We leaned against our compound wall wearing school uniforms: long-pleated skirts and white blouses. The sun rose with fervor while monks with shaven heads dressed in orange robes knocked on doors to receive rice porridge from my neighbors. The air smelled salty while pigeons converged upon scattered bread crumbs.

I felt a profound sense of freedom. Maybe I was better off without Hell?

The silence between my sister and me wasn't unusual. This time, we weren't speaking because of a recent fight. Mom had insisted we take self-defense classes after a stranger tried to pull me into his car.

I had stayed at the Church—too long after Bible—to finish homework. Thus, I ended up returning to campus through a back alley. All the other girls walked far ahead in clusters. I dropped my key chain and failed to realize I had stopped in front of a car with a window rolled down. As I stood up, I felt a man's greasy arms engulfing me. Luckily, I screamed so loudly that I was immediately released. I then ran to class as fast as I could. Not surprisingly, my teachers, classmates, and family blamed me. Everyone asked, "Why were you walking alone?"

Consequently, Kitty and I enrolled in after-school Tae Kwon-Doe. Being the ultra-competitive girl she is, my sister took the opportunity to pummel me. Apparently, "You bitch, I saw him first," and, "You want everything," aren't Tae-Kwon Doe commands. Suffice it to say; we were both immediately expelled, which hardly seemed fair since she'd started it.

A stray cat sauntered by while our neighbor returned home. According to rumor, Apple was the mistress of a high-ranking politician. This explained her colonial-style home and Benz. I admired Apple's pink Manolo Blahnik heels, which didn't quite match her orange polka-dot puffy cocktail dress. She waved at us. I smiled and waved back.

"Gosh, Kitty, do you think Apple partied the whole evening?"

I honestly couldn't care less. I'd grown up keenly aware of adult indiscretions. Thus, idle gossip never interested me. But I was eager to make amends with my sister. Kitty ignored me and jumped onto the bus in such a brusque manner that the door almost slammed in my face.

When we arrived at school, I sauntered to the back. I felt curious eyes upon me. As I opened my locker to retrieve books, Terry ran up and declared, "Fina, your boyfriend has been cheating on you."

I slammed the door shut. "Who?"

"Your boyfriend," Terry repeated.

"I don't have a boyfriend."

"What about Jack?"

I shook my head. "He's not my boyfriend."

"Jack says he is."

"The guy is quite the storyteller," I responded while walking away.

Terry chased after me. "Then why is Jack always with you?"

I stopped and, in an exasperated tone, replied, "Must I explain myself again? I let Jack carry my books and run my errands out of the goodness of my heart. If he wants to tell people I'm his girlfriend—well, I can't control what people fabricate, can I?"

"Really?"

"So much for being nice."

Terry's eyes widened. "You or him?"

"Me!"

"Yeah, well, I saw Jack making out with Tiffany."

"And why should this concern me?"

I marched to class.

Terry chased after me. "Fina, I know you."

I chose a seat by the window.

"Do you?" I asked while she slid into a wooden chair beside mine.

"You're sensitive."

I ignored Terry and flipped through my notebooks.

She continued, "That's why you play a romantic girl on TV. We all know your type."

"My type?"

"Yeah, your type always gets heartbroken, becomes hysterical, and ends up in an insane asylum."

I sighed. "That's a cliché, isn't it?"

"Huh?"

I leaned back in my chair and gazed out the window while my classmates piled in. "A trite plot."

Terry still didn't seem to understand. She continued, "Fina, you're a nice girl."

I smiled and quipped. "People see themselves in others."

I wished people didn't fixate on appearances. When you're a demon, you see through people quickly. I disagreed with the belief that one's appearance reflects one's soul. It's such a shallow and cruel judgment.

I buried my head in a book and laughed silently. If people only knew who I really was and how little I felt, maybe there'd be fewer rumors about my alleged sentiments. Then again, as Errol Flynn once said, "It's never what people say about you. It's what they whisper." I was too human for Hell, but too callous for Earth.

***

After morning prayer and Biology, I headed over to the snack bar. I ignored the faint whispers of classmates. Someone clutched an *Elle* magazine. I noticed my image on the back—it was an ad for lotion.

"Fina, don't you miss Jack?" Terry asked.

"What's there to miss?"

"An errand boy?"

I laughed. "Indeed. Well, he'll be back."

"How can you be so certain? He claims his compensation was poor."

"Youth is irresistible yet rarely satisfying."

Terry's forehead furrowed. "What are you talking about? You're only seventeen."

"Goodness, nothing," I replied, suddenly realizing I had accidentally shared the words of a former life. I did this sometimes luckily most people were too self-absorbed to notice.

I purchased a guava. Terry teased, "Fina, why do you always eat fruit?"

I was about to answer when I felt a gust of wind. I paused while my heart skipped a beat. There was an ethereal presence in the midst.

Quickly, I began wandering away.

I heard Terry mutter, "What's gotten into her?"

Someone else replied, "That's so Fina."

While pacing, I felt steps approach. I rapidly spun around. A man in a white robe stood in front of me. I gasped.

It was Raphael. Archangel Raphael was one of God's most trusted angels. While my brother Satan had traveled through chaos to get to Earth, Raphael went to warn Adam and Eve about his plans.

"Lucifina, how are you?"

"Quit the nonsense, Raphael. What are you doing here?"

In addition to being a messenger, Raphael also thought of himself as a teacher. In Eden, he spent much time trying to explain creation to the curious Adam and the events that had transpired in Heaven.

"Lucifina, it's been a long time," Raphael whispered. His soft skin was pale against his curly blonde locks. His blue eyes looked more turquoise in this light.

"Not long enough," I hissed while storming off. Just when I thought I was free of Hell, I was confronted by an angel.

"Lucifina, please wait."

"Raphael, I have to get to class." I heard the school bell ring, so I dashed away.

Bible was my least favorite class. It wasn't that I disliked the subject. In fact, I'd always been passionate about this ancient document. After all, it was the only book my parents didn't encourage me to read. Unfortunately, my teachers didn't like students who asked too many questions. And I had quite a few.

I was polite and smiled a lot. But people always wanted so much more. I'd grown accustomed to agents and advertising executives who insisted on controlling me. But it was never enough. It wasn't just respect everyone wanted; they demanded complete submission. My soul was my own, and I refused to give in.

CHAPTER 5: 90 MINUTES LATER

After class, I headed to my locker to switch books. Carly ran up to me and said, "Lucifina, I saw your latest television commercial."

"Which one?" I asked, smiling.

"You were wearing a pink gown."

"Ah, the air freshener," I responded while wincing at the memory of that job.

I'd been on the set for nearly eighteen hours and felt slighted by the makeup artist, who whispered insults. During takes, I'd fought to suppress bitterness while pretending to be a joyful girl at a party. I didn't care what people thought. However, I didn't appreciate being controlled.

"You looked so pretty," Carly continued.

"Thank you," I replied with genuine tenderness. "That means a lot, Carly."

"Fina, why are you always alone?"

I shrugged. "I don't have co-dependency issues."

"Huh?"

"Never mind," I replied and took off.

I've never been a joiner or a follower, which was my problem in Heaven and even Hell. Groups, no matter how benign, typically take on a cult-like mentality. If you're like me and have a strong sense of self, that's a guaranteed recipe for disaster.

While heading toward the campus gates, I observed clusters of girls congregated by the fence. They were generally friendly and welcomed me. Today, I couldn't stop. I scurried out of school, past the security guards, and down a dusty alley. I felt heavy footsteps approach.

"Lucifina," Raphael yelled.

He's back! I thought impatiently, reaching into my purse for a weapon. All I had was a mini squirt gun Mom bought to spray the cats with when they jumped on her furniture. I'd stolen it because I don't condone punishing any living creature but made exceptions for angels.

"Lucifina," the archangel repeated.

I spun around and squirted Raphael with the toy.

I kept squeezing the water gun until I heard Carly yell, "Lucifina, what are you doing?"

"Oh, nothing," I said, quickly hiding the device in my handbag.

"You were squirting water."

"Um, yes, a bug was attacking me," I quickly explained.

"A bee?" Carly asked.

"Sure."

"Spraying water won't do anything," she explained while walking beside me.

"I see. Carly, do you know how to kill an angel?"

"What?"

"An angel," I repeated.

"Like a Biblical one?"

"Yes, exactly."

Carly clutched a Bible against her chest. "Why would you want to kill an angel?"

"Oh, my goodness, I would never. It's just that I think this question might be on our upcoming Bible exam."

"Hmm, I don't think so."

"Oh, c'mon, you never know."

"True, Miss Tracy can be quite tricky."

My eyes narrowed as I analyzed Carly. My classmate believed what our teachers taught us. She didn't fake enthusiasm as I did.

"So, how do you kill an angel?" I repeated.

Carly shook her head. "You can't. God protects his angels. Only he can destroy them."

"Ah, okay," I replied quickly. "I have to go."

***

Raphael reappeared as I hurried down the busy street.

"Lucifina, I'm not a cat. You can't chase me

away with a water gun."

I ignored him.

"I thought we could talk."

"I have nothing to say."

"God wants to offer you amnesty."

I froze. "Why would I want *that*?"

Raphael's eyes twinkled. "C'mon, Luci, deep down, you know you're still an angel."

"Don't call me Luci," I snapped and stormed off.

Raphael followed. I was starving since I hadn't eaten enough. These days, I mostly ate fruit. I sidled up to a fruit vendor and made a selection. While the hawker pulled out a ripe slice of pineapple and began chopping, traffic rushed behind him. Black exhaust filled the streets while cars slammed on their brakes and blasted their horns.

Raphael stood beside me. "Luci, if you return to Heaven, you can eat as much fruit as you desire."

"What makes you think I want *that*?"

"God is all-knowing."

"Yes. He's worse than the Gestapo, the NSA, and every totalitarian government combined."

Raphael ignored my blasphemy. "Luci, don't you remember how happy you were in Heaven?"

I turned away and refused to look him in the eye. "That was a very long time ago."

"Yes, before Earth even existed."

I stopped for a moment while chewing pineapple. I analyzed the overcrowded buses trudging through the streets. I observed beggars and invalids with messy eyes and missing limbs.

Then I snarled, "Satan sent me to destroy the Earth, but it looks like you've beaten me to it."

"Now, Luci, let's not make false allegations."

"Oh, please, look around. Why did God create something only to have it rot?"

Raphael stood quietly. He was the consummate diplomat. Finally, he responded, "God works in mysterious ways."

"Trite platitude," I said flippantly. "At least Satan wants to destroy Earth quickly. Meanwhile, God is content to let its creatures suffer slowly."

I then bolted, but Raphael pursued. "Luci, it's not like that. I'm not sure if you truly know your brother."

"Not know my brother? Satan is my twin. I know him better than myself. We're one and the same."

Raphael shook his head. "You and Satan are fraternal twins. Yes, you share the same DNA. But you don't share the same soul."

I rolled my eyes. "Strange to hear an angel discuss genetics. I didn't know you supported science."

Raphael ignored me. "Luci, as of yet, you have no mortal sins on your soul."

I paused to reflect. I finished my pineapple and threw the sticky bag in a trash bin.

Raphael continued, "You love animals. In

Heaven, you could care for all of your friends."

"Do you scorn the ones in Hell?"

"The animals in Hell are skinny and wound-infested. They're suffering."

"And whose fault is that?"

"Must we assign blame?"

"How convenient that Heaven consists of only one percent of the universe."

"I wish that weren't so."

"So you say, yet look at your ridiculous entrance policies."

"Now, Luci, that isn't fair—"

I crossed my arms. "Convenient, isn't it?

"What is?"

"Sticking your nose down on us while Heaven hordes most of the wealth."

"We scorn no one."

"So, this is all in my head?"

"Luci, the Kingdom of Heaven is open to all."

I shook my head and laughed. "Indeed, we all have a chance, yet only the chosen few enter."

Raphael stared. "It's not like that."

"So, what do you want?"

"Your salvation," Raphael whispered.

"What do you want in exchange for your offer?"

Raphael paused and slowly swallowed. Finally, he pulled out a scroll and said, "The names of all of your assets."

"I knew it!" I ran as fast as I could to get away

from him. I wasn't about to betray my only brother and the other demons.

CHAPTER 6: A FEW DAYS LATER

It was Saturday, and I was backstage at a fashion show on top of Bangkok's World Trade Center. Glass windows surrounded most of the room so that I could look outside and see the gray-blue skies, parks, and towers throughout the city.

I sat in the corner, telling jokes. No one seemed amused. I glanced around, realizing that, as usual, I was the wildcard. Neither my height nor hour-glass shape met the industry's standards. However, I felt that my vivacious spirit and lively expressions were adequate compensation.

Over a year ago, Mom's co-worker loaned me *Fit for Life* by Harvey and Marilyn Diamond. The book encouraged eating fruit for breakfast, lunch, and even dinner. Since I was in Bangkok, eating fruit was easy. Thus, I replaced most of my meals with pineapple, watermelon, guava, and papaya. Accidentally, my weight dropped to 90 pounds, and I booked significant campaigns.

But it was hard to escape scrutiny. Classmates wondered why I didn't join them for lunch. If I went to dinner with friends, the only thing I could order was dessert. I started to withdraw. At modeling jobs, clients criticized my weight and questioned my controversial diet. Finally, after losing a catalog job, I was ordered to gain weight. So I started eating meals again, and the weight rapidly returned. Now, I was 110 pounds.

How did I feel about the weight gain? I was ambivalent. I liked feeling healthier and energetic. Further, I'd always admired softer figured women like classic Hollywood legends such as Susan Hayward or Marilyn Monroe. Unfortunately, neither the modeling industry nor the camera agreed. After all, the lens is arguably the cruelest weapon of our century.

The fashion coordinator handed me a pair of pants. When I emerged from the changing room and sat down for makeup, Chad joked, "Hey, Fina, what have you been eating?" I glanced up. Chad was nearby having his jet-black hair done. At six-four, the chiseled Eurasian didn't have to worry about his weight.

I sighed. "Fruit."

"Then why don't your clothes fit?"

"The designers shrunk them."

"Ha, sure."

Only three months ago, Chad and I had appeared in a magazine together. He was more agreeable, then. It had been a location shoot in a valley. Chad and I modeled against a rocky cliff alongside horses. At the time, I was ten pounds slimmer.

Clearly, this guy didn't value my personality, which was his loss. More Fina to love was a favor to the world, and if people couldn't love me for who I was, well, that was their problem, not mine. I ignored Chad and focused on reading *The Economist.* I hoped he'd go away. After all, skinnier girls surrounded us.

"What're you reading?" Chad asked.

I hesitated before responding, "According to this article, China's male population will explode in another decade."

"So, you've booked your flight?"

"What?"

Chad clarified. "Have you booked your flight to China?

"Why would I do that?"

"So you can have all those men for yourself."

"You're so not funny."

I returned to my magazine.

"C'mon, Fina, just own up to your desires."

"Own up to your own."

"Chad, it's obvious Fina is gay," said a tall, muscular male model named Jess. He was someone I frequently saw at the fitness club. We rarely had modeling jobs together since he was older and more of a body-builder type. At six-three, his dark hair and hazel eyes complemented his toffee-colored skin.

I exhaled. "Not that it's any of your business, but I'm not gay."

"Then how come you don't want us like the other models do?"

I raised an eyebrow. "What other models?"

"The fashion models."

I started laughing. "Male models? I've never seen any women talking to you."

Chad snorted. "You're blind."

"Imaginary models don't count," I joked.

"Ha," Jess retorted, "you're the one with imaginary friends."

I shook my head. "I have friends."

"Pen pals don't count, either," Jess replied.

"They're the best kind," I argued.

"Nope," Jess responded.

"Selina and Evelina are my friends," I countered.

Jess ignored this fact. "Hey, I saw your latest music video."

My lips crept into a smile. "Oh? I want to see it. How was it?"

"The way you dance is funny," Jess answered. He then started shuffling and mimicking the way I dance.

I was relieved when I heard Evelina bark, "Jess, you like ridiculous."

"I know," he laughed. "I'm copying Fina. This is the Fina dance."

"Oh, yeah," Evelina agreed.

My cheeks turned crimson.

"Why are you fighting with these guys?" asked Evelina's younger sister Selina.

Evelina and Selina were a couple of stunners. For years, I'd seen Selina in the same magazines and catalogs I appeared in. She was half-Thai and half-Swedish and unforgettable because of her high cheekbones, full lips, and wavy mane of copper hair. Selina's eyes were perfect almonds. It was impossible to get an unflattering photo of her.

One day, at a magazine job, I was startled realizing we'd work together. Selina was incredibly kind but extremely quiet. She had a cool air, so I was surprised when she invited me to her home. Evelina was equally attractive but possessed a different look. She had a less oval face, rounder eyes, and a perfectly coiffed pageboy.

Both girls took me under their wings and were determined to make me a more successful model—even if it meant being bossy.

"They started it," I explained to Selina.

"You shouldn't get so upset when the boys tease you," she replied.

I sighed. "I'm not upset."

"Then why is your face all red?"

"Allergies."

Selina laughed. "Yes, allergies. Like the time I had you over for a party. You ate clams, and your face got swollen. So we spent the rest of the night at the hospital."

"I was so embarrassed."

"I've always thought of you as a funny girl."

"Thank you, Selina. See, Chad, she thinks I'm funny even if you don't"

Chad rolled his eyes but then got distracted by a local supermodel.

Selina sat down beside me and said, "Do you know why you're not a top fashion model?"

"Because I'm barely five-five?"

"It's because you're 100% girl."

"My brain isn't."

"Do you know what you should do?" Evelina asked.

I shrugged. "No idea."

"Change your image," Selina suggested. "It's too clean, too wholesome, and too girly."

I was envious of Selina and Evelina insofar as they always landed the bad girl roles. Are the so-called bad girls that bad? They're usually guilty of trusting too easily. That was the case for Evelina, who played femme fatales in soap operas. In reality, she was a hopeless romantic who dreamed of marrying a prince and having children.

Meanwhile, I played sweetheart roles while silently crafting sardonic jokes. And I was a stone-cold realist not easily swayed by my feelings. I had no intention of marrying because no one was going to own me.

Strangers told me I was a good person. Yet I

was the one with a dark past. Sure, I'd never technically killed anyone. But I'd done much worse. Befriending people, gaining their trust, and then handing them over to be tortured and killed. Is this the work of a good woman? No, it's the machinations of a billion-year-old demon sent from Hell.

CHAPTER 7: A FEW DAYS LATER

It was 3:00 p.m., so I quickly finished scribbling notes before the bell rang. While my classmates rushed out the door, I heard my Bible teacher call, "Fina, can I have a word with you?"

I tossed my books into my backpack and approached Ms. Tracy's desk.

"Fina, will you attend Prom this year?'

I sighed. "Probably not."

"Why not?" she asked, tilting her head to the side.

I shrugged. "I have other plans."

She nodded. "Okay, Fina, but if you do attend, there will be a dress code."

"Uh, huh."

"Last year, your dress was too provocative."

"I'm not planning to attend this year."

Ignoring me, she continued, "It seemed that last year you removed your straps?"

I shook my head. "I most certainly did not. It

was a custom-made silk cocktail dress. There were never any straps."

"Well, your female classmates said they saw straps."

"They saw the hooks used for hanging the dress on a hanger."

Ms. Tracy's face contorted. In a harsh tone, she said, "Well, if you attend this year, you'll have to wear a dress with straps and one that extends past your knees. Your figure is too curvy to dress that way."

I clenched my teeth. "I already said—I won't attend."

"Dear, don't get snippy with me."

"Can I leave? I have an appointment."

Ms. Tracy nodded, but she looked annoyed.

I shook my head and took off. While walking home, Raphael appeared. We paced in silence because I wasn't in the mood for conversation.

Finally, I spoke. "Raphael, let's say I did wish to return to Heaven…"

"Yes."

"Would I be tortured?"

"Why would you ask such a thing?"

I sighed. "I'm guilty of treason."

Raphael nodded. "Yes, but God is merciful and forgiving."

I was quiet.

He continued, "Besides, you've displayed immeasurable loyalty."

"To Lucifer and the rebel angels?"

"If you can be loyal to your brother and his cohorts, then you can be loyal to God."

"I wish I could believe you," I whispered.

We stopped in the middle of the sidewalk. The sun beat down upon us. The sound of traffic overpowered our exchange.

Raphael clasped my hands. "My poor dear, damaged Lucifina. My heart's darling."

I removed my hands. "Damaged?"

"I remember the days in Heaven when your soul was pure."

"I'm not damaged," I countered. "And that was so long ago."

"Yes, over a billion years ago."

"Why do you think I'm damaged?"

Raphael's turquoise eyes glimmered. "Because you can't trust."

"And why should I trust you?"

"Lucifina, you've been fed so many lies in Hell. You don't know fact from fiction."

I shook my head. "That's not true. It's you and the other angels who create stories."

Raphael tilted his head to the side. "How so?"

"It's bad enough that in Hell, we live in poverty and suffer for eternity. In addition, you've won the propaganda war."

"Propaganda war?" Raphael asked with feigned innocence.

"Hell is blamed for all the world's problems.

In fact, we're guilty *only* of a rebellion against Heaven."

Raphael nodded but had nothing to say. I strode away. This time, he didn't follow. I knew I'd said enough. I'd called Heaven out, and God wouldn't like that. I probably wouldn't hear from Raphael again.

CHAPTER 8: A WEEK LATER

I had finally accepted I was on my own, and Satan would never return my calls. Then one evening, when no one was home, I sat in my bedroom listening to the sound of thunder erupt across the sky. I peered out my window and watched lightning strike a few times. Soon the city was drenched in a downpour. Rain battered against the roof while the trees shook against the screaming wind.

I sat down on my bed and was about to read Dante's *Inferno* when I heard a clicking sound. All the lights vanished, but my room remained just dim enough to still see. I hopped out of bed and entered the black hallway.

I crept into my mother's bedroom and opened the door to where she kept a flashlight. But when I flipped the torch's switch, I discovered the batteries were dead. I stumbled around and awkwardly made my way downstairs. We kept matches near the dining table, where a large candle sat on a cabinet by the window.

The storm howled while the rain continued its drumbeats on the roof. I was startled by the sound of a crash. I immediately tensed but relaxed when I heard Blackie meow. As I rounded the corner and entered the dining room, I observed the storm through the windows. Suddenly, I froze.

A menacing figure stood casually in the corner. In the dark, the intruder's eyes glowed red.

His eyes narrowed. "Lucifina, it's been a long time."

I gasped—even in the shadows, my archnemesis oozed charisma.

Beelzebub was not a good-looking demon, but few remembered this when caught under his spell. His charm compensated for his physical deficiencies. He had straight brown hair, blue eyes, and honey-colored skin. His body was almost too lean and too muscular.

I stammered. "I thought I'd never see you again."

"You almost didn't."

I pondered this for a while. "I take it you know about Raphael's recent visit?"

Beelzebub smiled but didn't say anything. I didn't trust him because there had always been sharp rivalry between us in Hell. Sure, he was charming to my face. However, I knew his consistent interest wasn't genuine. He despised me because I was Satan's twin. Beelzebub was my brother's right-hand man, but he not so secretly desired absolute power for himself.

I faltered. "I don't miss Hell and don't wish to return."

"Angels don't belong in Hell."

"I'm not an angel."

"You've never fit in."

I looked down. "I guess not."

"Are you still single?"

"Why do you care?"

Beelzebub smirked. "Just a question."

"I haven't found the wrong guy yet."

"Lucifina, you're surrounded by pedophiles and white-collar criminals."

"Yes, but there's always something right about them."

"Uh-huh."

"Where's the challenge in that?"

"Challenge?" Beelzebub asked with an eyebrow raised.

"Never mind," I replied.

"You're still pining for Belial, aren't you?"

"I am not," I protested.

I sighed at the mention of Belial's name. Memories of him were as vivid as if created yesterday. Belial was a lithe blonde with pale blue eyes and pasty, anemic white skin.

Beezebub took a few steps forward and laughed. "You never change, Lucifina."

"Again, why do you even care?" I paused.

"How is Belial?" I asked innocently.

"He's fine," Beezebub replied with irritation in his dark blue eyes.

"Does he ever ask about me?" I whispered.

"Nope, never."

I nodded but felt pain in my chest.

"What do you see in the bum anyway?"

"It's complicated," I explained. "Belial and I share the same values and goals."

"You're delusional," Beelzebub scoffed.

I shook my head. "Neither of us wanted war with Earth."

"Lucifina, you didn't want war with Earth because you're an angel at heart and will never be a true demon."

"I most certainly am a demon," I contested.

"Whatever," Beelzebub retorted. "Belial didn't want war with Earth because he's a lazy ass."

"Belial isn't lazy; he's a relaxed demon of leisure—like any aristocrat." Indeed, Belial looked like he belonged in a Renaissance painting. His skin was as soft and tender as a newborn's.

"Lucifina, you see what you want."

I blinked back with confusion.

Beelzebub declared, "You're in love with the idea of love, so you've dreamed up some illusory connection with a loser who doesn't give a rat's ass about anything except loafing around. Belial is nothing but deadweight in Hell."

"Belial is too sophisticated for you to ever

understand," I argued.

"Even if that were so, Belial already has a boyfriend."

"What?" I gasped with horror. *Could it be true?* "Belial isn't gay."

"Yes, he is, and deep down, you knew it."

I was quiet.

Beelzebub continued, "This is so you, Lucifina. You only like men who are completely unattainable."

Perhaps my nemesis had a point.

He continued, "You're always pining for some loser in Hell."

"So?"

"So, maybe it's not the guy you like."

"I don't know what you're suggesting," I replied.

"Maybe you miss Hell," Beelzebub declared.

"What's there to miss? Earth has plenty of Hell's misery."

"Yeah, but it's not the same."

"I don't miss Hell at all," I insisted.

"Yes, you do," Beelzebub continued. "Hell burns through your soul."

I exhaled slowly. "Alright, maybe it does. So what?"

The demon stared at me. There was silence, so we listened to the sound of the rain. The storm had finally calmed.

Beelzebub headed toward the door. "Lucifina, I have to go, but think about what we've discussed."

"Wait, you don't make any sense." I chased after him, but he was too fast. Within seconds, he had vanished.

Good God, I thought. Beelzebub was so peculiar. I wondered what he was up to because Hell didn't give a damn about me, not anymore. They'd all made that abundantly clear, so they must be angry about Raphael's recent visit. Their interest had nothing to do with me and everything to do with loyalty and trust. Satan and the rest of the board were scared. They were afraid I'd betray them. I sighed with relief and crossed my arms. It was nice to know that I, at least, still had some leverage.

Happily, I skipped upstairs to my bedroom. I crawled under the covers and slept soundly, knowing that Beelzebub would be back. War is never over. Predators always return just when you've forgotten all about them.

CHAPTER 9: A FEW WEEKS LATER

It was Friday evening, and I was back at the World Trade Center. This time it was for a different fashion show. Tonight, I wore flattering evening gowns. While slipping into a silver cocktail dress with a draped neckline, the female models around me clasped their hands approvingly.

"Oh, Fina, you look so beautiful," Selina said, putting her arm around my back.

"Yeah, so sexy," Evelina joked while shuffling around in her typical comedic manner.

"Thanks," I replied shyly. "But you know that's never the look I'm aiming for. I wish I were more androgynous like the other models."

"Then lose the girls," Evelina suggested.

"Easier said than done," I lamented.

Changing the subject, Selina said, "Fina, afterward we're all going to watch a movie on the top floor.

"We?"

Evelina pointed to Chad and Jess, who joined us in the corner of the stage. It would be another ten minutes before the show began.

"What're we going to see?" I asked.

"*A Walk to Remember*," Selina replied.

"Jess and Chad are okay with that?"

"Hey, why not? You love romantic movies, don't you little Fina?" Jess joked.

"Not really. I'm dying to see *28 Days Later*."

"Are you serious?" Jess demanded.

"For sure," Chad chimed in. "We all know what Fina's all about."

"And what's that?" Evelina demanded with her hands on her hips.

"Fina's into torture porn," Chad replied, laughing as he pretended to slap me with his invisible whip.

Selina rolled her eyes while Evelina playfully punched him on the shoulder.

"Absolutely," I agreed.

"Shhh," the fashion designer ordered. "Okay, Fina, you're on."

I heard Fat Boy Slim's *Right Here, Right Now* blasting.

So I took to the stage like I was Naomi Campbell. I didn't care if I was half a foot too short or ten pounds too curvy, I strutted like I owned the place.

While sauntering down the runway, I noticed a greasy-looking European ogling me. *Was he Beelzebub or my wild imagination? Stay focused,* I told myself. I swayed my hips to the side and smiled into the cameras at the end of the stage. The paparazzi were in full bloom. However, during every change, I couldn't help noticing the same man. Was he a demon?

After the show was over, I slipped back into my school uniform.

"Is that what you're wearing?" Evelina demanded.

"Sorry, I forgot to bring a change of clothes," I replied sheepishly.

"It's okay," Selina said. "We're *only* going to the movies."

"You look like a little girl in your uniform," Chad teased.

"I wish the modeling world agreed," I responded while the five of us pushed through the crowds to exit the backstage of the fashion show.

Jess shook his head. "The modeling world is filled with pedophiles. You're a real woman, Fina. Own it."

Just as Jess made that statement, the European I'd seen all night pounced on me. He engulfed my body like an octopus. I felt smothered.

Instantly, Jess grabbed the guy and pushed him. "Hey, get off her."

"Yeah, back off," Evelina yelled.

He took off running while I tried to catch my

breath.

"You okay?" Jess asked, putting his arm on my back.

I hugged Jess and exclaimed, "Jess, you saved me."

"No problem," he responded.

I continued, "A year ago, a man in a suit picked me up and carried me off in a crowded bus. I was screaming, and no one did anything. Finally, I broke free, ran off the bus, and hopped on another. But the guy reappeared. So I jumped off that bus and raced into moving traffic until I reached a motorcycle gang. They saw my fear and took me home."

At the time, I was petrified, wondering if my assailant was one of Hell's demons. I also felt sad, realizing that such an encounter had never occurred in billions of years because I was Satan's sister. Without his support, I was just another pretty girl no one cared about.

"What was that, little Fina? I couldn't hear anything you said. It's so noisy in this mall."

"Nothing Jess. I mean, thank you." Secretly, I was glad Jess hadn't heard my tale because it seemed too gushy. After all, I wasn't a damsel in distress or a victim. I was still a demon, just not one with any power.

"Yeah, sure thing kiddo. Anything for you."

PART 2: THE HUNT FOR AARON WALKER

CHAPTER 1: THREE YEARS LATER – SINGAPORE

Three years had passed since the fashion show, where Jess gallantly rescued me from a lecherous scoundrel. At the time, I had still been in high school. A few months later, I graduated and took a year off to complete modeling contracts in Hong Kong, Taiwan, and Bangkok. Subsequently, I moved to Eugene, Oregon, and completed two years of college.

In several weeks, I'd begin my junior year at the University of Oregon. It was the end of summer, and I was in Singapore completing a modeling contract because work was slow in Bangkok, where my parents still lived.

With trepidation, I walked to Elite Model Management, located within a colonial-style building, which was characteristic of the former British empire. Palm trees and hibiscus flowers distinguished this small island famed for cleanliness and organization. Alice, my booker, ordered I meet with her. Based on her tone, I knew this wasn't good. I entered the immaculate office. Model cards of striking women lined the walls. The agency was empty and felt dead.

So I sat down in a chair and began rifling through *Vogue*.

Eventually, Alice barged in. Her bones protruded through her sheath dress. She had a long neck accentuated by her short bob.

"Fina," she barked.

"Yes," I smiled brightly.

She sat down and scrutinized me. "Many clients have complained."

I looked down but didn't say anything.

"Can I see your new pictures?"

"Yes." I pulled out a large envelope from my beige satchel.

Alice rifled through the images quickly. "Fina, I told you to think about bunnies."

"I was thinking about bunnies."

"What?! No, your expression is too sexy."

"That's my normal look."

Alice groaned. "Fina, your look says 'I'll steal your boyfriend.'"

"But, I would never—" I protested.

"No one cares."

"Maybe it's time for those bad girl roles. After all, I'm twenty-one."

"Then you need to lose weight."

"I can't. All I eat is fruit."

"Then cut back."

"On fruit?"

Alice was impatient and looked annoyed. "Fina, I don't have time to argue with you."

"I was the region's highest-paid model for five years."

"Two years ago! You're over the hill now."

"I'm old?" I gasped.

She exhaled. "Yeah, I can't sell you for teenage roles anymore, and that was your strength. Now there's no place for you."

I stammered but couldn't think of anything to say.

Alice jumped up, dashed back to her desk, and retrieved an accounting notepad. "Fina, I'm cutting you a check. It's not much because you've hardly made anything this summer."

"Two television commercials, a cell phone print ad, and a fashion show," I reminded her.

"Yeah, but after you pay your flight, rent, and taxi fees for castings—all you have left is $500."

And agency cut, I thought. "I guess that's better than nothing."

"Now that's the spirit." Alice walked over, handed me a check, and shook my hand. "Good luck, Fina."

"Thanks," I said calmly.

I picked up my handbag, sadly strode out the exit, and returned to my studio apartment to pack my things. I whispered goodbye to my chain-smoking roommates. Two skinny brunettes lie sprawled out on our beds. They were hungover from a late night at Zukes, a renowned hotspot in Singapore.

I felt dead inside. It wasn't just the excruciating heat or termination from Elite; it was burn out. Remember those voices of former lives I spoke of earlier? I barely heard from them anymore. Maybe it was because I'd been on such a treadmill these past few years. There was hardly any time for reflection. At twenty-one, I felt so much older than my peers, whose eyes widened at the promise of alcohol. I'd grown up in a party town where anything and everything was easily accessible. By that logic, partying offered little appeal.

For billions of years, I'd felt a dichotomy within. I wasn't pure enough for Heaven, nor was I dark enough for Hell. If anything, I was a demon-angel hybrid. In the same manner, in this life, I was frequently torn between Eastern and Western ambiguities. I preferred to view the world as an outsider. It was a more objective approach. When you focus on what other people are thinking, it prevents you from becoming a victim.

CHAPTER 2:
BANGKOK

My flight from Singapore's Changi International Airport to Bangkok's Don Muang was reasonably uneventful. I mostly read *The Tale of Genji* because I felt irresistibly drawn to its sensitive, melancholy, and psychological aspects. It was haunting because I suspected I had lived portions of this book in another life.

When the taxi pulled into my compound, my heart skipped a beat as it did whenever I returned home. While entering the gate and hopping on to the porch, I could hear the bells chime.

I quickly opened the front door and entered the foyer, which was guarded by a black oriental screen. I stepped upon teakwood floors. To my left was the living room, where red silk chairs sat in the corners; opposite was a couch underneath a gold-trimmed mirror. A modest chandelier hung above a coffee table. Large cherrywood shelves filled with classic books and a Buddha statute separated the study and dining room. A door cut the rest of the house off from an open-air kitchen.

Lightheaded from the trip, I set my heavy suitcase on the floor. While walking toward the staircase, I passed the living room. I was immediately overwhelmed by apprehension. I felt an ominous presence. The scent within our home was typically floral. Now there was a pungent odor—it smelled like patchouli.

I shivered because I knew someone malevolent was watching me. My heartbeat quickened. I froze and turned my head. As I looked into the dimly-lit living room, I let out a scream of horror.

My sister's tall, lanky ex-boyfriend sat in the center of my mother's ivory sofa and stared at me with creepy confidence. He was not a good-looking guy, at least not in my opinion. Then again, I was biased. Herman had curly red hair, freckles, round green eyes, a big nose, and a rectangular face.

I was in shock. "Herman, what the Hell are you doing here?"

Suddenly the kitchen door swung wide open as Mom barged in. People said she and I looked alike, but I think they're joking. Mom had blonde hair, blue eyes, a pixie-shaped face, and a very skinny nose.

"Fina, why are you screaming?" she demanded.

I pointed at Herman. "Why is *he* here?"

"This is your sister's boyfriend, Herman,"

Mom explained.

"Ex-boyfriend," I clarified. "Kitty dumped this clown months ago."

"Fina, behave," Mom ordered. "This nice young man flew halfway around the world to spend the summer with us."

I felt dizzy. The room was spinning. Was this a nightmare? Whenever you think things can't get any worse, they can and do.

"Nice young man? Mom, are you insane?"

"Fina, stop it. You're the crazy one."

I stammered, "I'm crazy? He's a stalker who chased me across the world."

"Wow, you've emotionally regressed. You used to be so mature. Is everything about you?"

Herman continued to glare at us with a dark grin. He was enjoying our spat.

"Mom, why?"

"I invited Herman to stay with us because he's so heartbroken over your sister."

"The Hell he is."

"Fina, quit swearing."

"Why didn't you tell me?"

Mom's mouth tightened. "This is my house. I don't need your permission regarding guests."

I swallowed hard. "Mom, there's a reason why Kitty dumped this little punk."

"Yeah, because she's a heartless, cold-blooded sadist," Herman shouted.

"See," I said to Mom. "Nice young man, indeed."

Mom let out a heavy sigh of exasperation. "Maybe I should order dinner."

"That'd be nice," Herman yelled.

"How about pizza?" Mom suggested with a big smile.

"Do I look like someone who eats pizza?" I demanded.

"I'll order Hawaiian, and you can pick the pineapple off of it," Mom suggested.

"Whatever," I muttered while picking up my case and heading upstairs to unpack.

After ordering pizza, Mom followed me. "Fina, what's wrong?"

"Everything."

"Modeling in Singapore didn't go well?"

"I was cut," I replied.

"It's for the best. It's time for you to get a real job."

I was eager to change the subject. "Mom, do you understand why Kitty dumped el-weirdo?"

"Fina, please stop the insults and name-calling. It's not nice."

"Yeah, well, maybe I'm not a very nice person."

"Maybe that's why things aren't going well for you."

"No, it's because I'm old and fat."

"Fina, you're only twenty-one."

"Can we get back to Herman?"

"Yes, your sister broke up with him when she met Daniel."

I shook my head furiously. "Nah, that wasn't the reason."

"Then what was it?" Mom asked while she began adjusting my bedspread.

I started unpacking, but then stopped and exclaimed, "Mom, the guy broke into our house."

"Fina, don't embellish. From what I understand, he climbed in through a window."

"Yes, my roommate's window!"

Mom shrugged.

"He left vials of blood and strange poetry."

"Teenagers do peculiar things when they're in love."

"Herman is twenty-two."

"Fina, maybe if you weren't so hard on others, you'd be kinder to yourself."

I slapped my forehead. "I feel like I'm talking to a brick wall."

"Fina, stop it."

"Where is the creep sleeping?"

"In your sister's room," Mom replied.

"She'd love that. He'll have a field day in there." I shook my head, imagining Herman rummaging through her undergarment drawers. *Unbelievable,* I thought. *Sleeping under the same roof as that despicable pervert.*

***

Hours later, after dinner, I retrieved a satin nightgown and headed to Mom's room. After she was in bed, I bolted the doors and slipped in beside her. I slid a knife under my pillow. This was routine, regardless of Herman.

While my peers focused on self-awareness, I fixated on strategy. My motto is, "Every day is war." My philosophy is, "Never surrender. Fight until you die. Kill or be killed." The only thing worth living for is revenge.

There was no way I'd risk a wayward intruder entering our chamber. I was safer here than in my bedroom. I was paranoid that Herman would leap over my sister's balcony into mine, break the glass door, and then strangle me or worse.

While getting ready for bed, I confided in Mom, "I'm concerned about my skin."

"It looks clogged. I think you need exfoliation."

"Exfoliation?"

"Yes, try this new heating mask I bought."

I carefully applied it. "Mom, it's burning."

"Oh, it's supposed to have a tingling sensation."

"This is more than just tingling. My skin is on fire."

"Well, your skin is sensitive."

"I'm taking this off." Removal revealed a beet-red face.

"Oh, it'll go down," Mom assured.

"I hope so," I said while applying moisturizer. I then crawled into bed. "What does Dad think about our visitor?"

I knew my father well, and the last thing he'd want is a strange man in our house. My parents separated when I was seven. Dad lived near his factories in Chinatown but appeared regularly. Thus, it almost seemed like he still lived with us.

"Your father is upcountry on business. He won't be back for a month."

"He'll be furious."

"He has other concerns."

"Business is bad?"

"Yep."

I sighed, pulling the comforter over me. Business hadn't been good for Dad in years.

CHAPTER 3: THE NEXT DAY

The sun's powerful rays and birds chirping forced me awake. I crawled out of bed and analyzed my skin, which was bright pink and looked burned. Modeling would be next to impossible now.

I felt so defeated, but quickly washed and applied moisturizer and a heavy foundation. Next, I threw on a sundress and flew down the stairs. The house smelled like cinnamon and syrup.

As I stumbled into the dining room, I spotted Herman sitting at the dining table's head. He erupted into hysterical laughter.

"What?"

"You look like a tomato."

I winced. "Does Kitty know you're here?"

Herman shrugged. "She's probably with some guy."

"Hey, watch it," I snarled.

"Since when do you care about Kitty?"

"I don't, but what my sister does—what any

woman does—is none of your damned business."

Herman affected a sensitive, albeit fake, look. "Yeah, but I care about Kitty."

Liar, I thought bitterly. "Doesn't matter. You don't own her."

Khun Jai, our housekeeper, plowed through the kitchen door. She was a heavy-set woman with olive skin, round black eyes, and inky hair. She placed a tray in front of my enemy.

"Make yourself at home," I suggested.

"I am." Herman looked gleeful while eying his plate of pancakes.

"Fina, be polite. He is such a nice young man."

I sighed. "Khun Jai, if you only knew..."

"Knew what?" she asked.

"The things this guy has done," I muttered under my breath. But no one heard me, and I didn't think anyone cared.

Within seconds Mom entered.

Khun Jai raced to her side with a tray. "Madame, here is your breakfast."

"Thank you," Mom replied.

Mom happily sipped her scalding coffee and began slathering butter on toast.

I eyed Mom's fried eggs with disdain. "Healthy breakfast."

"We can't all be supermodels," Mom quipped.

Khun Jai shouted from the kitchen, "Fina, I

bought you a watermelon."

"Thanks, I'm not hungry," I grumbled while reaching for coffee.

"Maybe you'd be nicer if you ate more," Herman opined.

"Zip it, Herman."

"Fina, be nice," Mom pleaded. "Herman is our guest, so show some hospitality."

I glared at Herman. "Did you fund this trip with dirty money?" He swallowed his pancake and took a long sip of orange juice.

Mom piped in, "Herman works at a video store. We had a lively discussion regarding movies."

"Porn?"

"Fina, stop it. Herman was raving about *The English Patient.*"

"I'll bet," I said dryly. "Did he mention his drug dealing?"

"What?" Mom exclaimed.

"Isn't it obvious? Herman is a pothead."

"Fina, stop slandering our guest."

"Mom, just look at him."

Herman stared at me coldly from across the table. I stared back and crossed my arms. Tension grew as I refused to blink.

The silence was interrupted by a loud rustling noise. A black cat with white paws and a white-collar climbed up a tree, slipped through the window, and flew in.

"Captain Blackie in his tuxedo," I exclaimed happily. My mood shifted dramatically.

"Dr. Blackie," Mom corrected.

"Captain Blackie," I repeated. "After all, he flies as adeptly as any pilot."

Upon birth, I desired a cat, but my requests were routinely denied because Mom, like the rest of my family, preferred dogs. Maybe it was because they valued loyalty and obedience. Mom was a firm believer in education.

I accept people are born a certain away and can't be changed. I admired the graceful movement of cats. In nursery school, I stumbled upon a litter of kittens and moved them in. The largest of the three was Blackie—his brother and sister eventually moved out after Mom adopted more dogs.

At seventeen, Blackie seemed young for his age. He taught me many things: simply because someone tells you to do something doesn't mean you should; keep your distance; trust your instincts; owe no one anything; and always fight for your freedom.

"Fina, Blackie is now Maw Blackie," Khun Jai explained. Maw meant doctor in Thai. She placed half a watermelon in front of me.

Herman analyzed me.

"Why?" I asked.

Mom explained: "Our neighbor at the end of the street, Khun Yao, was choking, so Khun Jai went to help. She took Doctor Blackie. He let Blackie's toe beans stroke Khun Yao's throat for a few minutes. Soon the choking ceased."

"I see. Blackie is quite the miracle worker," I joked.

"Yes, Maw Blackie," Khun Jai added.

"Alright, or maybe Khun Yao was so startled by our cat's dirty paws against his throat that it distracted him," I suggested.

"Nevertheless, Dr. Blackie saved the day," Mom stated firmly.

I groaned. "Why can't I have a normal family? I used to think I grew up in a zoo. Now I think I live in a snake pit."

Herman sipped more juice. "Snake pit?"

I sighed. "It's a reference to an old Olivia de Havilland film."

Herman raised an eyebrow.

"It's about women institutionalized for insanity in the 1950s."

"I don't see any crazy women here," Herman taunted.

"Ha, ha. Incidentally, I still despise Kitty for moving a snake into our home in Oregon.

"Fina, stop calling Herman names."

"Oh, I wasn't calling Herman a snake. Didn't Kitty tell you?"

"Tell me what?"

"She bought a pet snake."

Khun Jai gasped. "Ai ya? Ngu?"

"Yes!" I said to Khun Jai. "Can you believe it?"

"Why?" she asked. Her black eyes broadened and her forehead creased.

Herman chuckled. "Your sister loves snakes."

"My sister loves to torment me."

"Your sister just likes to tease you," Mom countered.

I swallowed. "Kitty fed her snake live mice."

Mom gasped. "Oh, Fina, you've always loved mice."

"Yes, all rodents."

Mom turned to Herman and explained, "When Fina was young she rescued baby mice from our cats' mouths and released them into a field."

Herman smirked. A sinister look gleamed from his eyes.

Mom continued, "She had a pet squirrel named Nutty Nibbler and his siblings Tina Turner and Timmy Tiptoes."

"Interesting," my nemesis remarked snidely as if collecting useful data to wage against me.

Thankfully, we were interrupted by the phone ringing. I leaped for the phone and was relieved to hear Khun Jin's voice, "Fina, you have a casting. Can you go now?"

"Yes, absolutely," I said breathlessly.

"It's for facial cream."

"I love those jobs."

"Yes, Fina. Dove would pay at least $25,000."

CHAPTER 4: TEN HOURS LATER

My casting was a disaster. The makeup artist immediately whined about my skin and refused to apply makeup. The casting director suggested I return after my skin had cleared up. I was so humiliated. This had never happened before. My complexion had always been my selling point. The industry will overlook extra weight if a girl has good skin.

I tried to explain that my typically good skin was reacting poorly to environmental changes. Further, Mom loaned me a heating mask that created a massive breakout, redness, swelling, and broken capillaries. No one cared.

Khun Jin hadn't called yet, and I was worried. An advertising executive had been at the casting. This was rare. Generally, one doesn't meet the executives until callbacks or even the job. She had adored me a few years ago and insisted I'd be her future brand ambassador. Today, she'd looked so disappointed.

I returned home overwrought, but thankfully no one was around. Mom and Herman had gone out for fish and chips—not exactly diet food. Khun Jai always left before sunset. I flew up the stairs and into my bedroom. I fell on my bed and tried to read *Paradise Lost* but couldn't focus.

Finally, I stopped reading and hugged my pillow. I thought about my next move. I checked texts and was thrilled to hear from my girlfriends Evelina and Selina. They were excited I was back and insisted we meet soon to work out, go shopping, or have dinner.

I pulled out my laptop and scrolled through e-mails. I stopped to analyze the last one I had ever received from Jess. Remember the male model who teased me about invisible friends and said pen pals don't count? Well, believe it or not, after I started college, I heard from Jess. I didn't expect to ever hear from him, again. After all he was like ten years older, had a serious girlfriend, and was a notorious player. I wrote him off as the type of guy who is super flirty if you're in front of him. But out of sight, out of mind.

Once I started school, I focused on working and studying. Thus I hardly thought about the past. Then, one day, I was about to write a report on Karl Marx when I opened an e-mail from Jess. He messaged from time to time. Granted, they were fairly simple messages like:

Hey Little Fina, Wassup. It's me, Jess. Went to the gym today and had a few beers.

As a joke, I'd typically respond with novella-length, flowery e-mails. I told Jess all kinds of details about my life—like when I was upset about having to wear a shirt with a blue hen for a waitressing job. Or my essay on *Beowulf* for English lit.

Jess would write back: *K, all good,* or nothing at all.

I sighed. Either he didn't care about my essay on *Sir Gawain and the Green Knight* or the guy wasn't much of a pen pal. I suspected both. Then again, I never had any expectations.

Last Christmas, I visited Mom for two weeks. I was buying roasted bananas from a street hawker when I got a call from Jess:

He teased, "Hey, Little Fina, I saw you walking down the street."

"How did you know it was me?"

"C'mon, Fina. I'd recognize your walk anywhere."

"What's up."

"Not much, just calling to say hi."

"Thanks, maybe I'll see you at Clark Hatch?"

"Yeah, for sure."

I hadn't heard from Jess in months. I texted Selina, Evelina, and Chad and asked if anyone had seen or heard from him. They all laughed and agreed, "One of his girlfriends' probably murdered him. After all, he's such a player."

I sighed and decided to get ready for bed. Sleep was vital because I had the worst headache. I crept slowly to the bathroom.

Did it bother me that Satan never called or wrote? Absolutely. In a moment of rage, I e-mailed him and declared:

You're not my brother. I hate you. I'm now blocking you, so if you ever try to contact me, I won't know.

I suspect that Satan didn't care. After all, if he had, he could have found a way to communicate. And I don't mean through that dark varmint Beelzebub. What kind of twin sends such a rascal?

While showering, I heard a loud crash. I jolted alert and turned off the faucet. I blinked rapidly, listened, and wondered what it might be. Dr. Blackie on the prowl, I hoped.

A few seconds later, I heard a loud bang against the front door. I shivered. Was it Herman? I wasn't in the mood for his nonsense. Then I heard a click, the lights went out, and I heard a crash. The cat?

In the dark, I carefully stepped out of the slippery bathtub. Water dripped from my hair and body, so I reached for a towel and began anxiously patting myself dry. I threw on a cotton dress hanging on the door and tiptoed into the hallway to investigate. An eerie presence lingered.

The house was dimly lit thanks to the street lamps, which emanated light through the windows. I did my best to pretend I wasn't home, a falsehood that would be apparent to anyone since Vivaldi played in the background.

"Lucifina," said a baritone voice in the hallway.

My body stiffened, my lips quivered, and my hands trembled. I hadn't heard my real name in over three years. I missed it and was overwhelmed by euphoria mixed with sorrow.

"Lucifina," the tender yet deep voice repeated.

"Beelzebub," I whispered with fear, apprehension, and excitement.

I spun around, raced back upstairs, and slammed my bedroom door shut. But it was pointless.

Within seconds, the demon was in my room at the foot of the bed. The lights flickered on and off, so it was occasionally bright or subtly lit by the faint glow of the moon. I sighed, realizing the electricity hadn't gone out. Beelzebub was being his usual dramatic self.

"Lucifina," my enemy murmured. "It's been a while."

I gasped. "I didn't think I'd ever see you again."

Beelzebub did not move. I studied him carefully, realizing he hadn't changed. He was still as muscular and devilishly attractive as ever.

"You've missed us."

"Why would you think that?" I faltered.

"Your sorrow for Hell can be heard throughout the universe."

"I'm not unhappy."

"Then why can I hear your heart aching?"

"Because you're delusional."

"Simmer down," Beelzebub ordered.

"Don't tell me what to do." I bolted for the entrance, hinting that Beelzebub should leave. I started to open the door when he abruptly shut it tight with his hand.

"Lucifina, we need to talk."

"I have nothing to say."

"Get dressed and meet me downstairs," he ordered.

"I am dressed. I won't go anywhere with you."

Beelzebub stormed over to my closet and rifled through dresses. He pulled out a green satin gown.

"Wear this tonight, but first reapply your makeup. You need to be more presentable." He then strode out the door.

I was irritated by his arrogance and attempts to dominate me. *Some things never change*, I thought bitterly. In Hell, Beelzebub was always trying to usurp Satan's power while manipulating me. I'd almost gotten rid of this demon, but now, like a virus, he was back.

CHAPTER 5: 45 MINUTES LATER

I emerged in my emerald gown and walked downstairs to the dining table. Beelzebub was at the head. To my delight, the half-gallon of lily of the valley perfume I wore made him sneeze. I didn't bother to suppress my laughter.

"Jesus, Fina." He shot me a dark look before pulling out a manila envelope.

"What's in there?" I was genuinely intrigued.

Beelzebub grinned because he knew how to draw me out. I'd do anything for a story.

"Sit, Lucifina."

I sat down, thinking bitterly, *This demon has some nerve barging into my home, ordering me what to do.*

"You want to return to Hell, don't you?"

"Not really," I replied, looking away.

"Look me in the eye and say that."

I refused.

Beelzebub softened and said with more charm, "Take a look at these pictures." He then removed dozens of black and white photos.

I studied the images of victims, bodies maimed and burned.

"They were tortured?" I gasped.

"Yes."

"Why?"

"They were trying to overthrow the government."

"They look so young."

"They were. Many high school kids joined the movement. Most were university students and imprisoned for days. The girls were stripped naked while the men were beaten. A teenage virgin was raped to death by an angry mob. They plowed wood into her nether region. Finally, everyone was forced into a barren pit, where they were burned alive."

"Who?" I stammered, "did this?" My hands trembled, and I crossed my arms.

"Those in power, but there were outside forces."

Shaken, I paused to pour water into a glass from a carafe sitting on the table and then repeated, "Outside forces?"

Beelzebub nodded. He pulled out another photo and explained, "There was a specific man in charge of this operation. Troy Walker."

Anxiously I clasped the photo and analyzed it.

"He's old."

"Not as old as us."

"How do you know Walker is responsible?"

Beelzebub smirked. "I know everything."

You're not God, I thought. I wondered if this was one of Bub's elaborate stories. He'd always been a conspiracy theorist and loved pinning blame on anyone unlucky enough to cross his path. He'd done this for thousands of years.

I bit my lip. "Alright, so what do you want me to do?"

Beelzebub's red-bulging eyes narrowed. "Punish Walker."

I tossed the photos aside and leaped up from the table. "That's never been my job."

Beelzebub carefully stood up from his seat and followed me to the door. I walked outside for fresh air. I was overwhelmed by the graphic images. A breeze blew through my hair as the wind chimes hummed. I could hear cars rushing by and the soft meows of Blackie. I knelt and stroked his fur.

"Lucifina, you may have been a recruiter, but that was a long time ago."

I continued to pet Blackie, but then slowly rose to face Beelzebub.

"I was assigned to powerful men: Gaddafi, Kim-Jong-Il, and most recently Vladimir Putin." My job was to make these men loyal to Hell.

"Yes, and you failed every time."

His words stung like a rusty nail shoved into

a healing wound. I stepped back to get away from Beelzebub but then stopped. "Those men trusted me. I was their confidante."

I crossed my arms angrily. It was apparent that Beelzebub was attacking me because I threatened him. He was jealous of my relationship with Satan. All Bub cared about was power.

I was progressive and sought to soften Satan. I felt Hell needed a feminine touch. After all, there were no women on the board. If I were in charge, there'd be less aggression.

"Nope, they played you."

"They didn't. They never controlled me."

"Then why did you become sensitive to their side?"

I swallowed. "To know one's enemy, one must understand the enemy, think like him, and even become him."

"Face it, Lucifina. You lost your objectivity."

"I didn't."

"You sucked at your job."

"But I tried..."

"Effort is meaningless in Hell. We're 100% results-oriented, and you were bad."

"Then why was I in the field?"

Beelzebub smirked. "Nepotism is the only reason you got anywhere. You're Satan's sister."

I clenched my fists and ran back into the house. Beelzebub was on my heels, as was Dr. Blackie.

"This assignment is beneath me. I'm not an assassin."

"Too bad, Lucifina. This is your last chance."

I stopped, then pivoted.

"If I'm successful, can I return to Hell?"

"Absolutely."

"And I'll be reinstated to my former position?"

"Sure."

I softened and became more receptive.

"Lucifina, don't you want to see justice done to men like Troy Walker?"

"Yes, of course. So, where is he?" I asked, sitting down on a living room chair.

"Troy is in China. But his son, Aaron, will be in town this week."

"Son? Shouldn't we go after Troy?"

"Nope, you know how these things work."

"I guess."

Beelzebub continued, "It'd be too merciful to kill Troy. By going after the man's only son, we'll cause him unspeakable pain."

I shrugged. "Do psychopaths care about their children?"

"Troy certainly does. Aaron is his only son."

I got up and clutched my purse, which contained only my cell phone, some makeup, and cash.

We walked outside to catch a taxi.

"Where am I supposed to find this Aaron person?"

"He'll be at The Hibiscus."

"Good God, a casino?"

"You're hardly one to judge," admonished Beelzebub while hailing a taxi. We slipped in. I sat as far away from him as possible.

While the taxi drove through the back alleys, I stared out the window. I observed the dingy slums filled with shacks and children dressed in rags. The driver took a few sharp turns down a road littered with pot-holes until he entered the main road, which took us to the highway.

Soon we were blazing across the overpass, which showcased the city's skyscrapers and bright lights. We rode in silence, but I could hear the hum of folk songs on the radio. When we reached the waterfront, we exited the taxi and marched up the steps of the casino. The extravagance here was a stark contrast to the shanty towns around the corner.

I hopped up the steps. I could hear the clicking of my heels while lifting my dress to prevent it from dragging. I turned and looked for Beelzebub, but he shook his head.

"Beelzebub, aren't you coming?"

"Nope, you're all on your own."

"But how will I know who is Aaron?"

"Head to the main hall. Aaron is sitting at the poker table. Join him for a game."

"I don't know how to play."

"Then learn."

"What? What does Aaron look like?"

"Your friend Jess."

"What?" I stammered. I was utterly baffled, but before I could continue, Beelzebub vanished into thin air.

"Incredible," I thought.

CHAPTER 6: FIVE MINUTES LATER

I entered The Hibiscus, a notorious casino nestled at the edge of the river. It was renowned for gangsters, money-launderers, and international white-collar criminals. As my heels snapped against the marble, I analyzed the vast interior.

The chandeliers, red velvet, and gold trimmings seemed so ostentatious. The hall scent was a blend of cigarette smoke, whiskey, and chilled orchids. My eyes began to sting from the sudden dryness, which was a severe contrast to the humidity outside.

In the foyer, I glanced in the mirror and admired my reflection. My skin remained luminous. This venue felt so incredibly evil like a half-remembered nightmare. It reminded me of Hell, the home I so desperately longed for.

Someone tapped my shoulder and asked, "Excuse me, miss, can I help you?"

Startled, I practically leaped, but replied,

"I'm here to see Aaron Walker."

"And you are?"

"Fina."

"Please wait a moment."

I stood for a few minutes, waiting. I felt nervous, wondering if Aaron would bother to meet a random stranger named Fina.

"Please come with me," said the manager.

I followed across the crowded floor. Men in tuxedos threw dice across green tables while underweight women in tight satin gowns watched.

I felt shifty eyes glance in my direction. Certain glares scorched through my skin like iron blades.

I sauntered like I was on the catwalk—perhaps not a good thing. Fashion shows had never been my strength. There was a time when I almost fell off the runway. Part of my costume, a round plastic hat, had fallen across my face. Tonight, I was equally anxious. I almost tripped over my gown as the manager abruptly stopped at a table in the center of the room.

"Fina, please have a seat," the manager directed.

Awkwardly, I plopped down on a red velvet chair and found myself looking across from a man with a square jaw, muscular build, and dark curly locks. His hazel eyes flickered with danger. *This must be Aaron*, I thought.

A mixture of hatred and fear oozed through

my veins. Aaron reminded me of a northern barbarian from a Chinese soap opera. With his high cheekbones, deep-set eyes, and rugged appearance, he was like a combination of Genghis Khan and the Viking Leif Ericson. There was something eerily familiar about this man. Had we met before? Certainly not in this lifetime.

I must have shown my alarm because Aaron's serious demeanor suddenly transformed into a hearty chuckle.

I lowered my chin and eyes demurely. "It's nice to meet you, Mr. Walker."

He nodded but seemed surprised by my response. "How do you do?"

"Very well, thank you."

"Would you care for a drink?"

I shook my head politely. "No, thank you. I came to bring you a message."

"A message?" Aaron asked with a raised eyebrow. He then motioned with a jab of his wrist to summon the waiter who poured a glass of water.

"Yes, I represent Belle Venture Holdings. My boss asked if he could meet you.

I retrieved a business card from my purse and presented it to Walker with both hands.

Aaron shook his head, leaned back, and steepled his fingers. "Sorry, Fina...is that your name?"

I nodded. "Yes."

"I don't do business with strangers."

"I see." A slight quiver replaced my smile. I dug my nails into my palms before crossing them.

Aaron's eyes seared into mine. "Would you like to play a game?"

"What game?"

"Poker."

"I've never played before. Please be gentle."

Aaron burst into laughter and shook his head. He then distributed cards while continuing to hold his gaze.

My cheeks singed from the intensity of his stare. I could feel eyes from all across the room, scalding through the hollow of my chest.

Goosebumps grew on my arms. I compressed my lips before ravenously gulping a sip of water. I then opened my wallet and traded a few notes for a stack of chips.

Aaron remained laser-focused on his cards. He was eerily still.

I fumbled around, trying to figure out what I was supposed to do. A ten of hearts slipped from my palm and onto the table. Aaron peeked and grinned.

I quickly reassembled my cards and swallowed hard. The silence was uncomfortable. I was eager for conversation.

I babbled, "Gosh, this feels so much like that book by Fyodor Dostoevsky, *The Gambler*." Aaron raised his head and looked me in the eye. His poker face frustrated me. So I continued, "Have you read it?"

Aaron glanced back at his hand. "Nope."

"It takes place in a casino."

"Did you come here to tell stories or play games?"

"Both," I chirped while my lips extended into a wide smile.

"Did you want to draw?" Aaron asked while trading a single card.

I blinked rapidly and touched my neck. My opponent smiled. I swallowed. "Sure, two cards," I replied, passing back a couple for a new pair.

Aaron threw several chips in the center. Nervously, I matched.

"Ladies first," he teased.

"Checkmate."

He rolled his eyes. "Wrong game."

I displayed my cards: an ace, king, queen, jack, and a ten of hearts.

Aaron's mouth tightened. "That's a royal flush. I thought you said you've never played."

I shrugged. "Beginner's luck. What do you have?" He revealed three Jacks and two tens. "That looks good," I said.

"Yeah, it's a full house."

"Is it better than a…royal flush? Is that what you called it?"

Aaron exhaled, crossed his arms, and clenched his jaw. "Do you know how rare a royal flush is—especially for a beginner?"

"No idea," I stammered. I trembled because I sensed aggression. I sprung to my feet and began to dart away.

Aaron jumped up and followed. I could feel his heavy footsteps close behind mine. "Fina, I'm sorry. I didn't mean to upset you."

"It's okay."

He then clasped my wrists and remarked. "Your wrists are tiny."

Tersely, I retrieved my hands and declared, "Everyone is staring. Touching a woman's wrists in public is most undignified." I took a step backward.

"I see." Aaron chuckled and took a step forward. "So, a woman like you coming to this part of town alone isn't?"

I gasped and began to turn. Aaron stepped in front of me.

"Everyone is watching us."

Aaron nodded and replied, "Yep, they are."

"I should go." I turned to leave, but Aaron followed.

"Wait, Fina, you forgot your chips."

I paused to accept them.

"Let's play another game," he suggested while escorting me to a booth where I exchanged my chips for cash.

I hesitated. "I don't really like poker."

Aaron laughed. "Another game then."

I thought for a moment, but then joked, "Well, I'd love to arm wrestle."

Aaron was exceptionally broad-shouldered and muscular. He raised an eyebrow while analyzing my upper arms, which were small in length but soft and feminine.

I continued, "Can we play chess?"

"Um, yeah, if you want to join me in the study upstairs."

My body stiffened. "Gosh, I don't think that would be a good idea."

"Why?" Aaron tilted his head to the side.

"We've only just met. It's not proper."

Silently, I considered. This would be the perfect opportunity to slice Aaron's throat. But I was concerned about security. This place had more guards and cameras than Alcatraz.

"Okay, let's go to the terrace. The manager will bring a chess set. There'll be plenty of other patrons. Then you won't feel scared of being alone with me."

"Scared?" I placed my hands on my hips. "You should be afraid of me."

Aaron laughed. "Alright, thanks for the warning."

***

Aaron and I now sat opposite one another at an outdoor table overlooking the river. The scent of jasmine overpowered the terrace. A faint flurry of stars hovered in the distance.

The manager brought out a chess-set and

placed it between us. Aaron leaned back in his chair. "Ladies first."

I blinked rapidly, analyzed the board, and then moved a pawn forward. Aaron mirrored my move.

"Fina, you were telling me about your company earlier."

"Yes," I replied. "My boss is looking for new investments."

"Why casinos?"

"It's different."

Abruptly, the manager interrupted and whispered in Aaron's ear.

"Fina, I'm sorry. I have to take this call."

I stood. "I should leave."

Aaron shook his head. "No, it's okay."

"It's getting late. My mother will worry. I really must go."

"Oh, okay, I'll call you."

"Sure, it's on the card I gave you," I said and scurried out of the casino as fast as I could.

I ran out to the taxi cue, where there was no line. I was hopping into a taxi when Beelzebub slid in beside me. We rode mostly in silence.

While exiting the highway and driving through back alleys, where the slums were now asleep, I spoke. "I know what you must be thinking."

"Why didn't you kill Walker?" Beelzebub snapped.

"The man is a savage, but he's refined and intelligent."

"So what? All you had to do was kill him."

"There's something so familiar about Aaron."

Beelzebub shook his head and stared out the taxi window. We passed a collision involving a tuk-tuk. "You have a wild imagination, Fina."

"Have I met him before?"

"No," he stated matter-of-factly. I could never tell when Beelzebub was lying.

I sighed, paid the taxi driver, and bounced out of the car with Beelzebub in tow. We stopped in front and whispered so as not to wake Mom or the neighbors.

The wind chimes clanged against the cool breeze. Dr. Blackie was wide awake and out on the prowl, evidenced by his military crawl position. An unsuspecting moth was the target.

"Beelzebub, I couldn't kill Walker tonight. It wasn't the right time."

"Right time?"

"I feel like there's information to be ascertained."

"No! No, no, no!" Beelzebub bellowed, jumping up and down with frustration. "Lucifina, you were given an order, and once again, you disobeyed."

"Yes, but there was security everywhere. Aaron is huge. There was no opportunity to kill him, especially since he had a call. Instinctively, I knew to get out. Otherwise, he'd have tossed me out."

"Oh, okay," Beelzebub replied, suddenly more understanding. "Alright, you did the right thing."

"Thank you," I said with more reassurance. "I'm certain Aaron will call me and there'll be a better opportunity to murder him."

Beelzebub nodded in agreement. "Goodnight, Lucifina."

"Goodnight," I responded. I walked through the gate, stepped onto the front podium, and entered home.

As I crept across the living room, toward the stair case, I observed Herman passed out on the couch.

Gross, I thought. While nearing the steps, I suddenly tripped over a shoe. I was furious while stumbling over and crashing against the dining table.

"Hey, huh? What's going on?" asked a drowsy Herman.

I nursed what would certainly be a bruise on my shin.

"Fina?"

"Go to sleep, creep."

"Where were you?"

"None of your business. Learn to put things away." I then tossed Herman's dirty shoe at him but missed. It crashed into Mom's beloved statuette of Yang Kwei Fei.

"Huh?" Herman murmured while falling back asleep.

I silently sobbed, watching the porcelain figurine shatter into pieces. I figured I could blame it on Herman. Maybe then he'd be gone. Why was he sleeping on the couch anyway? Wasn't my sister's bedroom good enough for him? Talk about invading everyone's territory. First, it was my home in Eugene, and now it was my parents' entire house. When would it stop?

I ran upstairs and showered to erase the memory of cigarette smoke, alcohol, and pure evil. I thought about Yang Kwei Fei. She was the favorite concubine of a seventh-century Tang Dynasty Emperor forced to sacrifice her.

While sliding into bed next to Mom, I analyzed this evening's events. Walker represented everything I hated. How dare he look at me the way he did? With such confidence? It was as if he could read my thoughts, and all it did was make him laugh. I quickly fell asleep, fantasizing about the way I'd torture and murder him.

CHAPTER 7
SATURDAY

The next day, I woke incredibly happy and excited. The sun rose with fervor and shone brightly into Mom's bedroom. Blackie slept soundly next to my feet. I practically bounced downstairs to the breakfast table.

Khun Jai was bustling about, refilling Mom and Herman's juice and coffee cups. The two devoured their French Toast like a couple of shipwrecked sailors who hadn't eaten in three entire days.

I slid into a chair, poured myself juice, and smiled.

Mom put down her newspaper and glared at me. "Fina," she demanded. "What do you have to say for yourself?"

"Huh?" I asked, reaching for a banana from the centerpiece. I carefully peeled and nibbled its sweet flesh.

"What happened to my statute of Yang Kwei Fei?"

I shrugged. "Herman broke it."

His face contorted. "No, I didn't. Fina threw a dirty shoe at me, missed, and broke the statute."

"I don't remember that," I lied.

"Yes, you do! You stumbled into the house smelling like an ashtray after midnight," Herman countered.

"Where were you?" Mom asked, suddenly forgetting about Yang Kwei Fei.

"I'm twenty-one and support myself independently. I don't have to explain my whereabouts."

"Fine, alright," Mom agreed. "But what about my statute? You know how much she meant to me."

I shrugged blithely. "If Herman hadn't startled me, I wouldn't have tripped over his dirty shoe. If I hadn't felt irritated by his presence and slobby behavior, then I wouldn't have gotten angry and thrown it at him—which he deserved. Besides, the statute is just an example of materialism."

Mom's forehead furrowed. "It's always someone else's fault, isn't it, Fina?"

"Thank you for understanding."

"Don't throw shoes at people—it's so rude," Mom lectured. "Show some hospitality and quit blaming people for your problems."

Herman shook his head, which caused Mom to ask, "What?"

"Do you know what Kitty has to say about

Fina?"

"We don't care!" I shouted.

"Fina, don't raise your voice. I'd love to know what Kitty thinks."

"Good God," I moaned.

"Kitty and I spent a lot of time together," Herman bragged.

I rolled my eyes. "You wish."

"We spent a load of time in Mom's basement —watching TV crime marathons during breaks," Herman continued.

"Yeah, that's why you're a zombie," I replied.

"All the murderers shared similar qualities," Herman explained.

"What's your point?" I demanded.

"Fina, you're a psychopath. Look at you. You're obsessed with cleanliness. You freak out about lint on your blouse. You nitpick your portfolio pictures."

Finally, Mom intervened, "Herman, I'm a neat freak. I have OCD. Am I a psychopath?"

"No, Marie, you're not because you have a kind heart. You care for others. You have compassion."

Mom nodded.

Herman continued, "Every person has imperfections. Everyone except Fina. She *seems* flawless."

"Is that a crime?" I demanded in a haughty tone with my nose in the air. "Is it against the law to strive for perfection?

Herman rolled his eyes. "You're so full of yourself. No, it's not a crime to be perfect, if you are. But you're a poser, a fake, a phony. It's a lot of work to cover up your genuine nature."

"And what nature might that be?" I taunted.

"Who do you care about?" Mom demanded. "Do you care about anyone?"

I pondered this challenging question for a moment but remained silent.

"Yeah, she cares about herself," Herman snapped.

I shrugged. "So what?"

"Are you even capable of feeling anything? Do you have real emotions?" Mom asked.

I stood up. "Of course I do. What a silly question."

"Not so silly," Mom retorted.

"If I don't feel, then why do I express emotions for the camera so well? Look at my pictures, television commercials, and music videos. I speak without saying a word."

"So what, Fina. Psychopaths and sociopaths are masters at feigning vulnerability—when it's convenient. They fake it so they can manipulate their unsuspecting prey," Herman explained.

"Well, then, which is it? Am I a psychopath or a sociopath?"

Herman downed his juice. "The former, because psychopaths know what they're doing is wrong. They just don't care. You're incapable of guilt."

"I love animals," I protested.

Mom shook her head. "Doesn't mean much."

"Yeah," Herman chimed. "Plenty of psychopaths and serial killers love animals."

"I thought they torture small creatures," I countered.

"Yes, very often," Mom agreed. "But Hitler was a vegetarian."

I sighed and jumped up from the table. "I'm tired of this absurd conversation. It's trite and boring."

"Spoken like a true predator," Herman observed. "They're always bored and hungry because they're empty inside. They only feel alive when they're about to commit an act of savagery."

"You'd know, wouldn't you," I snapped. "Anyway, even if I am a psychopath, so what? Why is it anyone's business except my own whether I feel or not? I'm so sick of people wanting so much from me. You're all a bunch of soul-sucking vampires. Maybe focus on yourselves and your sordid flaws."

Suddenly the phone rang. I leaped for the phone and was relieved to hear Khun Jai's voice. "Fina, you have a casting. Can you go now?"

"Yes, absolutely," I said breathlessly. "Where? What product?"

"X Studio on Soi 99. It's for shampoo."

"Wonderful," I exclaimed. I had deliberately grown my hair long for a shampoo advertisement. This was a gig I'd always wanted but never achieved.

I hung up the phone and asked, "Mom, can you drive me to my casting on Soi 99?"

"Sure," Mom replied. "Then we'll go to the grocery store."

"Yep," I agreed, racing up the stairs to grab my portfolio and a change of clothes.

Herman followed us to the car and crawled into the back seat.

I sat next to Mom while applying makeup. When I finished, I opened my book.

"Fina, what are you reading?" Mom asked.

"*The Tale of Genji.*"

"It's Japan's most definitive work of art," Mom conceded.

"And the world's first novel," I added.

"I'm so glad you're reading Japanese literature," Mom confessed.

"Why?" I asked suspiciously.

"Japanese women are so lovely. You could learn a lot from them and try to emulate their behavior."

My blood boiled, and I clenched my teeth. "Yeah, that would make a lot of sense."

I could see Herman mocking me through the mirror.

Mom glanced at me for a split second. "Fina,

what are you getting so worked up about?"

"I'm not Japanese—not even half, so why the Hell should I act like I am?"

Herman piped up. "I love Japanese women."

"Shut up, Herman" I shouted.

Mom shook her head. "That's exactly what I'm talking about."

I looked out the window and muttered, "Unbelievable."

"I spent my summer before my junior year living in Tokyo and loved it."

"How nice," I said smugly. "I wish I'd gone to Japan for the summer."

In reality, I'd had the opportunity to model in Tokyo when I was eighteen. However, I'd turned the contract down because fruit in Japan is extremely expensive, and I wasn't interested. Yet I was now irresistibly drawn to Japanese literature and perplexed by Aaron, who looked half-Japanese. Why? Was this connected to one of my ancient former lives?

"Hey, you're here for the summer," Mom snapped.

"Yes, I'm here to work my ass off. I need to make money since we're broke."

Herman interjected, "Quit whining, Fina, modeling is glamourous."

"Ha, the Hell it is, and mind your own business," I shouted.

"Fina, lower your voice," Mom admonished

as she pulled out of Soi 54 and turned onto Sukhumvit road. "Why are you reading something so archaic?"

"It's elegantly written—hypnotic and melancholy. It's about loss."

"Like I lost Kitty," Herman grumbled.

Serves you right, I thought bitterly.

"So much romantic stuff isn't healthy for you, Missy. If you want to understand Japan, I recommend *Shogun.* I learned more from James Clavell's best-seller than I did from an entire semester studying Japanese history and philosophy."

I shook my head. "*Shogun* isn't taught at university."

"So, what? I liked it," Mom retorted while narrowly missing a collision with a motorcycle as she turned onto the highway. "Have you even read *Shogun*?"

"Only the first 150 pages, but I'm put off by the sex."

"Because you're a prude," Herman taunted.

"Shut up," I ordered.

"Reading contemporary books would help you, Fina," Mom suggested. "You need to know what's going on in the world."

"Literature provides insight into the human mind," I replied.

"Wasn't *The Tale of Genji* written by a courtesan who never saw the world?" Mom asked.

"Lady Murasaki was a highly educated

woman and critical of the Heian courts; it's hierarchy, hypocrisy, and mistreatment of those without power. You say you're a communist. But Clavell was a hard-core libertarian and die-hard capitalist."

"I need to focus on driving," Mom said while speeding up against a truck on the highway. "Don't forget, I'm taking you to *your* casting." She glanced in the rearview mirror and then gripped the steering wheel with one fluid gesture.

"Fina, you've got some real hang-ups."

"Herman, please stop-talking."

"I know what your problem is…"

"You!"

"You need a man," Herman chanted.

"Mom tell this creep to shut up; otherwise I'll strangle him."

Thankfully, we were now driving off the highway and back on to Sukhumvit road.

"You know, Fina, I'd be happy to set you up on a date with my buddy Pete. He's got a great gig as a pot-dealer and is very experienced, if you know what I mean." Herman tried to catch my eye in the mirror to give me a knowing wink.

I was too disgusted to look the perv in the eye. "I wish you'd stop talking and drop dead."

"Pete knows how to please a woman."

"Alright, I've had it," I screamed. "Mom, stop the car!"

"But, Fina, I'm driving."

"Then pull over," I ordered.

"Okay, okay," Mom said with exasperation. "But you're blocks from the casting."

"It's fine; I'll walk," I insisted as Mom pulled up to the curb. Her car heaved as she jerked it to a complete stop.

"Fina, meet us at Villa when you're done," Mom suggested.

"Okay, thanks Mom," I said, jumping out of the car. I grabbed my purse and portfolio, but before shutting the door, I hissed at Herman, "Go to Hell."

"We'll go together," he joked.

I then hopped onto the soot-covered sidewalk and began walking in my heels rapidly to my casting.

The sun stung my skin since I wore a sundress. I felt drips of perspiration develop in my hair and neck. While scurrying to my casting, I observed fruit and snack vendors watching. Given the intensity of my expression, they probably thought I was black-hearted.

I tried to shade the sun with my hands while walking past palm trees and turning the corner on to Soi 99. The casting studio was at the end of the street.

Rage against Herman consumed me. I wished Mom would just drive him to Khao San Road –– throw him in front of a Hostel and drive away like I'd suggested earlier. Now it was too late. The worm had slithered his way into our lives and wouldn't leave.

There was only one thing to do — kill Herman. Approaching my casting, I felt infinite happiness while dreaming of how I'd kill the rat. A smile grew across my face while fantasizing about my favorite torture methods. But suddenly I thought, *Ah, the best way to kill vermin is with rat poison. I love rodents, but Herman is not a cute, cuddly creature. He's a dirty insect.*

I was now prancing up the tile steps of the casting house. While bouncing across the porch, I saw familiar faces of casting directors.

"Fina," said Khun Chompoo, "how lovely to see you!"

Khun Cherie clapped and said, "Welcome back."

"Thank you," I replied with the biggest sweetest smile I could affect.

"Fina, we have the perfect role for you."

"Really?"

"Yes, for this shampoo television commercial. We want you to play an angel."

"Ah, how suitable," I said with a sly grin.

CHAPTER 8: TWO AND A HALF HOURS LATER

I left the casting feeling ecstatic. Would this be my big comeback? The makeup artist had been so pleasant while applying makeup. My hair was silky today, as opposed to ashy. Thus, it was manageable and easy to set.

There were hardly any other models, so the wait time was less than ten minutes. I felt confident and posed with ease for snaps in the middle of the room while standing on white paper directly in front of the camera.

For the video, I began by saying my name, height, weight, proportions, and ethnicity. Then I role-played the part of an ethereal angel washing her hair.

After the casting, I flew into the street, hailed a cab, and took off for Villa grocery store on Soi 11. I pranced past vendors selling orchids, roses, and lilies. Blended scents lingered in the air. I Then turned into the European style market and spotted Mom in the bread aisle because her blonde hair stuck out like a ballerina in an artillery store.

"Hey, Mom," I said casually.

"How was the casting?" she asked.

"Good. Listen, I'll just be a second. I need to grab something."

"What?"

"It's personal." I crept through the back of the store toward the aisle filled with knives. When I reached the end, I spotted rat poison.

While examining the shelf filled with vermin killer, I felt hungry eyes upon me. I glanced up and spotted a devilishly handsome stranger wearing a University of Texas shirt. The tall, broad-shouldered man studied me carefully with a confident grin.

He started to approach, smiled, but then walked away.

I snatched a generic brand of rat poison and rushed to the cashier. Mom and Herman were standing in line, so I joined them.

I looked over and saw the stranger standing in the next line watching me again. I peeked at him shyly. He stared back, so I batted my eyes and quickly turned away.

After paying and collecting groceries, we stepped toward the exit. I noticed the stranger struggling with his two jugs of water. Considering his bulging triceps, this was unexpected.

I abandoned Mom and Herman, approached him, and asked, "Hi. Do you need help?"

"Ha, ha, you want to help me?" He stared into my eyes and chuckled.

"Sure," I replied.

He then jokingly extended one of his water cooler-jugs.

I attempted to clasp one, but he immediately pulled the jug back, roared with laughter, and took off.

Abruptly, I heard Herman's whiney voice croak, "Fina, what are you doing?"

I stammered, watching the athlete head out the door, "That guy kept looking at me and was struggling. I thought he wanted my help."

"Are you blind?"

"Kind of. That's why I'm dependent on bi-focals and contact lens. I also need vision therapy, but it's expensive. So, unless I get more modeling gigs, I can't afford it."

"Fina, you're such a nerd."

"You ought to crack a book for once. Why is helping someone nerdy?"

"He's obviously a college swimmer or a professional coach. Didn't you notice his overly developed lats and torpedo build?

"So?"

"So? You emasculated him!"

"How?"

"Ugh, Fina. You live in a bubble and are so used to aristocrats in Asia or leftist feminist men in the Pacific Northwest that you don't understand real men."

"Excuse me?"

"Real men," Herman repeated.

"Are you referring to yourself?" I asked snidely.

"Maybe, Dad is Russian, and I grew up in Boston."

I rolled my eyes. "Good God, Herman. Is everything about you?"

I brushed past Herman — deliberately shoving him hard in the shoulder. I waltzed over the ramp and strolled into the parking lot. I noticed Mom putting groceries in her trunk. I suppose I should have helped, but couldn't be bothered. She then dashed into O'Malley's, an Irish bakery at the end of the parking lot.

"All about me? Fina, you are the most self-centered egotistical bitch on the planet. Everything is always about you."

"Oh, yeah, Herman? Then why are you always talking to me?"

Herman blinked. "You're not a nice girl, Fina."

"Then go bother a nice girl and leave me the Hell alone!"

"Yeah, I've been thinking about doing that."

"Good. I am... we are all tired of you." I was

so busy arguing with Herman that I failed to notice the paparazzi inching behind me.

Mom sidled up to us and said, "Oh, stop fighting, you two. I bought a sheet cake." She opened a box revealing a beautiful white cake covered with vanilla frosting and pink roses.

I was so angry I could barely speak. I hadn't eaten all day, so my blood sugar was incredibly low. I desperately needed orange juice, pineapple, or roasted bananas.

Had anyone thought about me? No! All anyone thought about was themselves. I was sick of everyone's selfishness.

If Mom cared about me, she would have bought me fruit. *Then again, I could have purchased my own instead of wasting time looking for rat poison and flirting with swimmers. But that was beside the point.*

From the corner of my eye, beggars in rags hobbled by. One had a missing limb and clutched a rusty crutch. A kinder person would have softened at the sight, given these meek souls some money, and simmered down.

But I was hardly a role model. Instead, I thought bitterly: *How dare she buy cake? I can't eat it.* So, I grabbed the cake, scooped out a handful, and wiped it across Herman's face.

The beggars' heartsick eyes widened with alarm. Both looked famished, evidenced by their emaciated bodies and protruding bones. They probably desired cake and wondered why I wasted perfectly good food.

Mom was horrified and screamed, "Stop it, Fina. What are you doing?"

I ignored her and began reaching for more cake. I grabbed handful after handful. I kept smothering Herman with cake until he looked like a snowman in March.

Why didn't Herman react? Either he was in a state of shock. Or he enjoyed having my hands all over him and knew we were being filmed.

I was so focused that I barely noticed the cameraman surrounding us. The flashing lights and cameras clicking wouldn't stop.

"Fina, stop it," Mom wailed.

I looked up and saw a cluster of photographers snapping our pictures. There were even videographers and local news reporters. They'd captured my entire erratic explosion.

CHAPTER 9: THREE DAYS LATER

It was Tuesday morning, and I was at my modeling agency –– a modest townhouse on the other side of town.

I sat opposite of Khun Jin, who was behind her desk. Like most agents, she was very slender. The fluorescent lights glistened across her coffee-colored skin.

When I turned eighteen, I severed my four-year contract with the most prestigious agency in town. My former agent, Khun B, required exclusivity. At the time, agents fought for me. Thus, three years ago, Khun Jin's ebony eyes flickered with delight when I joined her. Today, those same eyes narrowed with disappointment.

Five newspapers cluttered Khun Jin's desk. In the corner, a small TV showcased my recent shenanigans. The local channels captured me smothering Herman with frosting. Khun Jin said nothing while sorting through papers and switching off the set. She leaned back and studied me.

I crossed my arms. "I can explain."

"Really?"

"It's…it's not me," I stammered.

"She looks like you."

"I swear. She's someone who looks like me."

"I see."

"Yes, and she's trying to destroy my image."

"She's doing a good job because right now your image is a joke."

"Yes, well, everyone says I need to change my style," I countered.

"Uh-huh."

"People complain that I'm a goody two-shoes. I'm boring."

"The fashion industry wants cool."

I tilted my head. "This wasn't cool?"

"Not at all."

"Didn't my casting go well?"

"Yes, the clients loved you. They booked you."

My chest filled with a burst of energy as I sat upright. "That's wonderful! This is the comeback I desperately need."

"Then they canceled."

"Why?"

"Why? Why?" Khun Jin glared at me. "Come on, Fina—don't ask why. You're supposed to be a brand ambassador. You need to be an angel, a role-model, and someone people look up to—not someone who throws a temper tantrum and wipes cake all over a guy."

"Sure, I get that, but Herman is a creep and deserved it."

"Maybe, but that changes nothing."

My lips quivered. "What'll I do?"

"Explain your side of the story to the media. Maybe people will feel sympathetic. Perhaps the public will relate to your passion. But right now, your career is over."

CHAPTER 10: THAT EVENING

After hours spent in stationary traffic, I was tired when I arrived home. So I ran up the stairs and headed to my bedroom. I switched off the light and fell on my bed, consumed with racing thoughts.

This is all Herman's fault. If he had never come, I wouldn't be so angry. If he hadn't provoked me, I wouldn't have lost my temper. Oh, how I hate you, Herman. If I weren't so busy, I'd march into my sister's room and murder you now.

However, I was too exhausted, so I started to nap but was startled by an angry voice.

"Quit whining, Fina. Quit blaming others and take some personal responsibility."

"Huh?"

I was instantly alert, sat upright, and found myself staring into Beelzebub's red, menacing eyes. He sat on the pink cushion of my peacock chair.

"What the Hell are you doing, Fina?"

"Getting ready to kill Herman."

"Have you completely forgotten your assignment to kill Walker?"

Now I was wide awake. "Oh, my God. Aaron...I completely forgot about him."

"Forgot? How could you forget?"

I shook my head. "I don't know. I've just been so busy."

Beelzebub gave me a disgusted look. "Yeah, busy fighting petty, useless squabbles with your Mom and Herman. Busy flirting and dreaming about strangers at grocery stores. And busy committing career suicide."

"That's not fair," I protested. "I didn't dream about that swimmer. Sure, I smiled at him, but I've been too busy with this media scandal to give the athlete a second thought."

"You've completely missed the point."

I sighed. "Look, I only just met Aaron Friday night."

"It's now Tuesday."

I shrugged. "So, what? It's only been four days."

"Shouldn't he have called by now?"

"Good God, Beelzebub. You sound like a woman going through a mid-life crisis."

"Don't mock yourself. You're how many billions of years old?"

I hopped out of bed and headed downstairs to fetch a banana.

When I returned, Beelzebub was reading *Wuthering Heights.*

I asked, "What should I do?"

"Call Aaron."

I shook my head. "Absolutely not."

"Why?"

"Then he'd have all the power."

"Fine, keep some leverage. But you're running out of time."

I swallowed. "Let's wait a few more days."

***

By Saturday, Aaron still hadn't called. Ordinarily, a week wouldn't seem like a big deal. However, I felt pressured by Beelzebub and anxious to solve the mystery of who Aaron might be. Beelzebub was lying, so it was pointless to press him any further.

I crawled into bed and began fluffing my pillow. Tense, I tossed and turned. I was drifting to sleep when the loud beeping sound of my phone startled me. My heart skipped a beat. Who could it be? I rolled over and checked. Much to my surprise, it was a text from Aaron.

Aaron: *Hey, how are you?*

It was 1:30 a.m. I decided not to respond since it was so late. Why was Aaron texting at this hour? Not a good sign. I fell back asleep.

When I woke at 7:30, I texted back: *Good, but couldn't sleep. How are you?*

Immediately, he replied: *Great. I'm headed to meet a client for breakfast. Why couldn't you sleep?*

Me: *I started reading Shogun but switched to Jane Eyre.*

Aaron: *I've read Shogun.*

Me: *Oh, wow. That's so cool. Shogun is Mom's favorite book so I've put it off.*

Aaron: *James Clavell spends a lot of time on research and the books are well written.*

Me: *Yes, have you read all his work?*

Aaron: *Tai Pan and Noble House. Dad wanted me to read King Rat but never got to it.*

Me: *I've only read King Rat.*

Aaron: *I'm walking up to meet a client. Will hit you up later.*

I jumped out of bed, showered, and started dressing. While skipping downstairs to get breakfast, I received another text.

Aaron: *Hey! Did you want to grab lunch today?*

This invitation was very last second, so I debated whether to put him off. I didn't respond while thinking. Before I had even poured coffee, another text appeared.

Aaron: *I won't be in town much longer.*

I felt frustrated because I didn't particularly appreciate his impatience. Why was Aaron suddenly in such a hurry? Then I thought, *Maybe I can push him into the Chao Phraya River.* I loved swimming, but in my experience, super muscular men do not. Aaron would surely drown.

I wrote back:

Sure, I can squeeze in a quick lunch. But I'll have

to leave early. I have plans.

Aaron: *How about lunch on our riverboat?*

Me: *Noon?*

Aaron: *Yeah. Need me to pick you up?*

Me: *Thanks, but I live on the other side of town. Traffic is insane. I'll leave now. It'll be faster.*

Aaron: *Okay, see you soon.*

Immediately, I downed a cup of coffee and flew back to my room. I changed into my favorite white dress and white hat and dashed back downstairs.

"Hey, where are you off to?" Mom asked. She was sitting at the dining table, reading *Robert's Rules of Orders.* She was obsessed with policy and procedure.

"Yeah," Herman chimed in. He was lounging on the couch, looking his typically vacant self.

"Off to meet Selina and Evelina for lunch," I lied.

"Where?" Mom asked.

"Downtown."

Mom removed her reading glasses. "Fina, you've still never apologized."

I paused in my white heels. "For what?"

"What you did to me," Herman whined.

"I know I hurt you, but you deserved it."

"That's not an apology," Mom declared.

I dashed to the door. "What do you want me to say?"

"Sorry," Herman suggested.

I exhaled. "Look, I've suffered enough. I lost the shampoo campaign."

"Serves you right," Mom said.

"Mom, we desperately needed the money," I reminded her.

"You're so self-destructive," Herman opined.

"I'm so sick of your opinions."

"Fina, you're not going anywhere unless you say you're sorry."

"Fine, I'm sorry Herman made me angry."

"Try again."

"Mom, I'm sorry I destroyed your beautiful cake."

Mom sighed. "Okay, be back by four."

"Why?"

"We're supposed to have dinner with Roxanne and Tom Barger."

"Count me out."

"Alright," Mom conceded. "You're a big girl."

"Indeed, I am." I then bounced off to catch a taxi.

Mom was right—I was an adult. Thus, I didn't appreciate having my schedule dictated by others. Nor did I enjoy being told what I should or shouldn't read. People intent on dominating others lacked personal self-control, which was why authoritative types didn't impress me. No one owned me, and I owed no one anything. Now, I had a mission: I needed to kill Aaron Walker.

CHAPTER 11: 45 MINUTES LATER

Before reaching the casino, I texted Aaron: *Almost here.*

He immediately responded: *Ok. Down in a second.*

While hopping out of the taxi, I spotted him running down the steps toward me. He was ruggedly athletic.

I suppose I should have exercised restraint and remained still while waiting for Aaron to reach me. However, I was neither demure, nor were my mannerisms affected. Thus, with girlish enthusiasm, I bounced over to meet him halfway. My heart quickened while loose-swept hair brushed against my rosy cheeks. I felt exceptionally warm as the sun beat down.

"You were fast," I remarked as Aaron barreled up to me.

At six-four, he seemed immense. At five-five, I felt buxom next to most locals. I was more like a '40s pinup girl than a fashion model. But in contrast to Aaron, I felt petite.

"Huh?" he asked with a big grin.

"The way you flew down to meet me."

Aaron nodded. "Nice hat."

"Thank you." I was wearing the biggest white hat I'd ever seen. Combined with my white dress and heels, it presented a classic look.

"Are you hungry?"

"Sure," I replied nonchalantly.

"Let's head this way to the boat." He extended a hand while leading the way.

I pranced in my heels as we strolled to the boardwalk. The rotting planks creaked. Aaron walked slower, almost behind me.

Neither of us said anything while we stepped into the medium-sized boat. It was a unique vessel distinguished by teak paneling, jasmine garlands, and periwinkle silk seating. The scent of chilled orchids permeated the interior.

The Chao Phraya—or River of Kings, as a former King had called it—looked deceptively calm. By the banks, children played in muddy-colored water while slow barges transporting cargo coasted upstream.

Finally, to break the silence, I asked, "Is it just the two of us?"

The attendant seated me at a dining table in the middle of the boat. Meanwhile, Aaron sat opposite me.

Aaron smiled. "Yep, and the crew."

I nodded, but I silently wondered how I'd throw my host overboard. However, I relaxed realizing witnesses wouldn't be a problem. The attendant would nap after lunch while the driver focused on navigation.

I'd create an accident—make Aaron groggy by slipping poison into his cocktail. Then I'd lean over the railing, pretend I'd lost an earring, and ask him to retrieve it. That way, he'd fall over without me pushing him.

I sighed with glee. This was almost too easy.

Aaron noted my mischievous yet satisfied countenance. "You look awfully happy."

"Oh, well…" I stammered. "It's rare I get out."

"Why not?" He tilted his head.

"I'm like a vampire and prefer the night."

Aaron nodded. "What do you do for fun?"

I didn't answer while analyzing shacks in the distance. They contradicted the luxurious hotels, condominiums, and temples. The sloping riverbank was a chaotic paradox.

I was lost in thought and didn't hear Aaron tease, "Shopping?"

"Good God," I protested. "I'm not that type of girl."

"What type are you?"

I tossed my head back flirtatiously. "The type that can't be trusted."

"Thanks for the warning."

"You're welcome. What type of guy are

you?"

Aaron leaned forward and grinned. "I'm just your ordinary, average guy."

I batted my eyes. "Yet you're so exotic."

Due to his height, Aaron gazed down at me. Thus, I had to look up, which I wasn't fond of because it made me feel vulnerable, and I needed to keep the upper hand.

A puzzled expression crossed his face. The intensity of his stare caused me to tug the collar of my neck and strands of hair. Under the table, I crossed and uncrossed my legs.

Aaron leaned back and steepled his hands. "I bet you say that to a lot of men."

"Maybe." My cheeks reddened because I had exposed myself. "But with you, I'm genuine."

He shook his head. "You're funny."

"Thank you. Most people don't get my humor."

"They're idiots."

I blinked furiously as I felt his eyes scorching my skin. Never in a million years did I imagine I'd meet a man who appreciated my dry wit.

"Miss, would you care for a drink?" the attendant asked.

I was grateful for the interruption. The boat was now chugging at full speed. Water splashed while I observed other boats, shop-houses, bars, and restaurants along the inky bank.

The attendant poured water and offered

wine.

I shook my head. "No, thank you. I don't drink alcohol."

"Oh, no?"

"Never."

"How come?"

I shrugged. "I have to watch my figure."

"What were we talking about the other evening before we were interrupted?"

"We were playing a game."

"Ah, yes," Aaron noted. "Seems you like games?"

I sipped water. "Chess is like international relations, don't you think?"

The waiter began scooping rice and vegetable dishes onto our china.

"How so?"

Nervously I babbled, "Well, you know the various analogies: zero-sum game versus the prisoner's dilemma."

Aaron crossed his arms. "I didn't study that stuff."

"The former supports a survivalist approach."

"Kill or be kill?"

"Yes."

"And the latter?"

I swallowed. "Cooperation."

"Didn't you approach me on behalf of a VC?"

"Oh, yes," I replied while shoveling broccoli

into my mouth.

"Your boss wants to invest?"

"Sure."

"What kind of money are we talking about?"
I bit my lip. "A substantial."

Aaron's tone was harsh. "We don't work with VCs. Hate them."

"Why?" I asked, feigning innocence.

"Me, personally?" Before I could reply, he passionately explained, "Our group doesn't want outside interference, management, or control.

I nodded. "That's understandable."

"But I've always hated bankers."

I nodded but looked down at my plate. I'd hardly eaten.

"I can relate," I replied.

"Oh, yeah?"

"It's a long story involving my dad," I explained, feeling vulnerable again. I looked away and watched the boats pass.

Aaron suddenly softened and tried to catch my eye but couldn't. "Your dad?"

I took a sip of water. "Yeah."

"My dad's a vet."

"Really, which war?" I asked, looking up and glancing into Aaron's.

"Vietnam."

"Oh." I was surprised by Aaron's candor. I had plenty of Eurasian friends whose fathers were in Vietnam, but most didn't discuss it for a variety of reasons. For example, I thought Jess's dad had been in Vietnam, but we'd never discussed it.

"Dad was in Asia for ten years."

"I went to school with kids whose dads were in Vietnam." I wasn't sure this was true. Many of my classmates were mixed, and their dads were military. However, had they seen active combat?

"Oh, yeah, were they weird?" Aaron asked with a twinkle in his eye.

"Weird?"

He ignored my question. "When Dad came home from the war, he was a mess."

I nodded.

"Dad lost a leg."

"How?"

"Landmine."

I nodded.

Aaron continued, "He's falling apart."

"Agent orange?"

"Yeah."

"That's too bad."

Aaron crossed his arms. "I didn't exactly have a Norman Rockwell upbringing."

"Me neither."

"Growing up, we moved around a lot. Mostly rented. Never owned a home."

"Okay."

"Finally, Dad managed to save up. So, we bought a real house."

"Cool."

"But damn, we missed one payment. That's all it took, and the cops were at our door threatening to evict us."

"Oh, no."

"So Dad argued that if we got evicted, then the house would be overrun with homeless who'd trash it."

I sipped some water. "Smart."

Aaron continued eating. "Dad negotiated the interest rates, which had fluctuated out of control. That's why we couldn't afford the payments. Damned usury system.

"I think the same thing happened to us," I whispered.

"Huh?" Aaron asked, motioning for the waiter.

"Since I was eleven, we've lived in a townhouse in a good part of town. Yet Mom insists Dad has never made any payments."

Aaron raised an eyebrow. "That's odd."

"Dad spends a lot of time dealing with his lawyers or in bankruptcy courts."

"Oh, yeah?"

I felt embarrassed, realizing I'd shared too much. So I asked the waiter for some coffee. Then I changed my mind. "Actually, can I have some wine?

"Really?" Aaron laughed.

I nodded. "This conversation has stirred me up. I need to calm down."

"But you said you never drink."

"I don't." I gulped the wine after the waiter poured us each a glass.

I reminded myself to stay focused. I surreptitiously retrieved a vile of powdered sleeping pills from my purse, which I planned to slip into Aaron's glass.

"Cool."

"Did your Dad regret Vietnam?"

My interest amused Aaron. "Dad was military."

"Yes, but a lot of vets have regrets."

Aaron smiled.

"Did yours?" *Does Troy have any regrets? Now's your chance, Walker. Maybe, just maybe, I won't kill you. At least not today.*

Aaron tilted his head and leaned back.

What is this? Some kind of game? His silence, coupled with his pleased look, annoyed me greatly.

Stridently, I asserted, "I supported the North because I support the rights of indigenous people."

Aaron's eyes widened. "That's funny. You don't look indigenous."

"I'm not."

"I was wondering what you are."

"Really?"

He stared at me. "Will you tell me?"

"My father's family is Teochew."

Aaron's forehead furrowed. "What?"

"A very ancient group. Through altars, our line dates back to the seventh century, when the

LICIA FLYNN

Tang dynasty flourished. While your ancestors pillaged villages, mine were drafting poems."

I knew I was being incredibly obnoxious. Was it the wine? Or had Aaron wound me up with his steady, silent demeanor? Instead of showing the requisite humility of a genuine lady, I was fired up like a banshee trapped on an Irish moor.

Aaron's eyes narrowed, and his smile vanished.

I continued babbling like a parrot. "Throughout the world, it's the natives who are exploited and hunted like wild animals."

Aaron didn't say anything. The twinkle in his eye returned. He evidently found my passion amusing.

I repeated, "So did your dad have any regrets?"

My target leaned back. "Like I said, Dad was military."

What kind of answer is that? In other words, Troy isn't human? He's just a machine—a hired gun? A paid killer who must be punished by making his only son suffer.

There was a glimmer in Aaron's eye. He was clearly enjoying my haughty interrogation. Did he ever interact with women who asked questions?

"I see," I said coolly. I contemplated how I'd sprinkle poison into Aaron's drink.

"Dad was fighting communism. He was fighting for *your* freedom."

I clenched my jaw. "By killing the natives?"

"My mother is indigenous. See my hair?" He ran a hand through his thick locks.

I shrugged. "I thought your curls were from your Western roots."

Aaron shook his head. "My Dad isn't racist because Mom is Japanese."

I felt frustrated because men often argue they're not racist because they've married a minority. This is a myth. Many hateful men do what's convenient. Many of my Eurasian friends were quick to point this out. Some frequently warned me about *sinofiles*—men with an Asian fetish. Was Aaron in denial about this reality? Did he even care? Or maybe he was genuine? Or was I jealous imagining that his father might have had some knight complex, rescued his mother, and maintained a healthy relationship? Meanwhile, my parents were divorced. I wanted to say racism and marrying outside one's race aren't mutually exclusive, but I bit my lip. Instead, tilted my head to the side. "Was your mother also from a military family?"

Aaron beamed. "Yep, my grandfather was a ship engineer."

"Then you're from a better class than I am."

"Oh, yeah?"

"I'm descended from a long line of merchants."

"Businessman?"

"There's an old Confucian saying: *Never trust anyone in business*."

"I don't."

"Nor I." My eyes narrowed.

Aaron laughed. "At least we agree on something."

In a snide tone, I continued, "I suppose I wouldn't be alive if it weren't for the Vietnam war."

Aaron was completely stoic. "What are you talking about?"

"It's a long story, but it's how my parents met." Technically, my father's family profited from the Vietnam war, but no one needed to know this vital piece of hypocrisy. Why focus inwardly when we can attack outside opponents?

With a smug smile, my enemy replied, "See, Fina, things happen for a reason."

"And you wouldn't be here if your father hadn't been sent to Vietnam, right?"

"Probably not."

I sipped more wine.

Thankfully, Aaron also drank more wine.

I remarked, "You seem very fond of your dad."

"Yeah, he used to take me hunting—"

"Hunting?"

"Yeah, we'd hunt—"

I put up a hand. "Please stop, I don't want to know."

"Okay."

"Can I use your bathroom?" I asked abruptly.

"Sure, it's over there." While Aaron turned to point out the washroom in the corner of the boat, I sprinkled powder in his wine.

Then I waltzed over to the lavatory. The intensity of our discussion had overwhelmed me. I almost liked Aaron because we shared certain experiences. Thus, with considerable effort, I reminded myself to stay focused. I needed to punish those responsible for killing the people I cared about. And more importantly, I needed to return to Hell.

I studied myself in the mirror and whispered, "Fina, don't let his charm distract you. Aaron is a cold-blooded psychopath like his father."

His glances created an equal proportion of anger and excitement. Such arrogance. How dare he look at me like that? He had to be punished. If I didn't throw Aaron overboard now, I might never get another chance.

When I returned, the waiter was clearing plates. He was about to serve a tempting dessert: fresh mango and sticky rice. Tipsiness vanquished me. No doubt it was the wine. I was relieved to see Aaron's glass empty. So, I clasped mine and downed what remained.

With a wide grin, Aaron chuckled. "Wow, for a woman who never drinks, you're a natural."

"Indeed, kind of like poker," I boasted.

His smile vanished. I felt tense, realizing I had said the wrong thing. I felt hot and reached for the bottle of wine. There wasn't much left, but I deftly poured the remainder into a glass and took a swig.

Aaron leaned forward. "No need to be embarrassed about your talents."

"Talents?" I asked nervously. I compressed my lips while placing my wine glass back on the table. I was drowsy but stared at the glasses, realizing something was wrong. "Wait! Was that my glass I just drank or yours?"

Aaron wiped his neck. I guess he was also feeling the afternoon heat. "Mine. Yours is the one with lipstick stains."

I froze. My heart quickened while my head tightened. I stared at the thick red lipstick stain covering the perimeter of a glass with my fingerprints. I'd swallowed my own poison.

Aaron was completely still. If we were in a jungle, his composure would make him almost invisible. In contrast, I began to tremble. It was an incredibly humid afternoon, but I was now shivering. I blinked rapidly.

Finally, to break the silence, I declared. "Oh, my God! The waiter must have moved the glasses when he was stacking plates. I didn't notice mine— the one covered with lipstick -- and accidentally drank yours."

Aaron laughed. "It's okay. Not a big deal. You're an interesting woman."

I wobbled, trying to stand up. "I bet you say that to all the girls."

"Maybe. But with you, I mean it."

Aaron had recycled my line, but I was too flustered to discuss it. I tried to breathe but had trouble inhaling. I touched my neck and paced to the center of the boat. Drowsiness consumed me. The room was spinning out of control. I almost tripped but caught the railing.

"Hey, careful," Aaron ordered while leaping up and moving closer to me.

But he was too late. I was dizzy and could barely stand upright. As I stumbled forward against the table, I heard the loud crashing of porcelain plates and silverware. I clasped the table cloth and felt my hand touch something—cold and squishy. Everything became blurry. I fell to the ground and hit my head against a chair. The room became black as I faded to sleep.

***

It's the eleventh century, and I'm sitting in the courtyard at the Imperial Court. I feel the sun's warmth while rays highlight the pink sky.

I write in my diary:

As Fall approaches, the leaves turn orange. The grass fades to copper and the banks by the stream dampen. The days shorten while the air chills.

I dislike court life because it's lonely and inadequate. I feel helpless and trapped.

My heart burns with agony because I yearn for freedom.

Members at court see me as stand-offish. I wish there were fewer drunken men here. Some love too freely. They are easily manipulated, only to be abandoned and left with sorrow.

While writing in my diary, I feel hungry eyes upon me. I carefully look up and am startled by a shadow in the bushes. I spot a Samurai lurking in the shadows.

Goodness gracious, what is he doing here? The eleventh century is a peaceful era. The Samurais of Clavell's Shogun don't exist yet.

He's so strong compared to my effeminate compatriots. He doesn't belong here—yet neither do I.

The Samurai catches my eye. I stand and take a step back while he takes a step forward. I turn to escape while his powerful steps approach. His movements scare the birds, so they dive into the cherry blossom trees.

I trip, but then hop to my feet and gather my long flowing robes. I begin to run as fast as I can to return home, but the walls are paper-thin...

There is no protection.

***

Where was I? Was I still asleep?

I tried to open my eyes but couldn't. I guessed I must be home in bed—with Mom. How did I get there? What had happened last night?

I wrapped my arms around Mom. It felt good to hug her because I'd been awful lately.

Wait a minute. Something wasn't right.

Mom generally felt soft. She had plenty of extra padding. But now she felt hard and muscular.

Why did I smell a masculine scent? Was this a new cologne Mom selected? It didn't suit her. I thought she should stick to floral fragrances.

I heard a deep voice whisper, "Oh, baby, you're so cuddly."

Bright lights appeared, but only for a split second. My pulse quickened while my eyes stung. I realized I was lying in Aaron's arms.

Startled, I screamed, "You're not my mother!"

I immediately pull away and determined we were in the back of a moving vehicle. My head was throbbing. It was dark, so I could barely see anything except for Aaron's wide grin.

"I am not your mother. Fina, you've got issues."

"That's the understatement of the year," I declared. "Where the Hell are we?"

"Do you remember anything?"

"Nothing."

"You passed out."

I backed into the corner. I felt an equal proportion of fear and rage. *Where are we going? Am I being kidnapped?*

"I'm so thirsty," I confessed.

Aaron opened a bottle of water and handed it to me.

"You created quite a scene back there."

"I did?"

"While fainting, you pulled down a table, broke china, and splattered mango across the room. The poor waiter was covered in coconut sauce."

"Good God, I'm so sorry." I felt my cheeks turn red.

"I carried you into the car. We're taking you home."

"How do you know where I live?"

"I called your mother using your cell phone."

"You did?"

"What was I supposed to do?" Aaron asked.

"How did I end up in your arms?"

"You forced your way into my lap and started fondling me."

"I did?"

"You even tried to kiss me."

"I would never," I protested.

Aaron chuckled and waved a finger. "Never say never."

"You've attacked my honor."

"What honor?"

I gasped. "What honor? How dare you!"

Aaron laughed. "Do you always talk like this?"

"Talk like what?"

"Like you're on stage."

I swallowed. "Occasionally."

"You're quite theatrical."

"Insulting me again?"

"I meant it as a compliment."

"Really?" My tone softened.

"You could be an actress."

"You, too."

"An actress?" Aaron asked with a raised eyebrow.

"I meant actor. You look like a Hong Kong actor."

"Thanks, I get that a lot."

"My parents don't want me to act," I confessed.

"Why?"

"They think it's silly."

"Sure, I never watch TV. It rots the brain."

"My father wants me to be an engineer."

"What do you want?"

"I've always dreamed of being a comedian."

"Seriously?"

I shook my head while the car turned into my compound. It rounded past the security box and drove toward my townhouse at the end of the cul-de-sac.

"Fina, I hope it's okay if I drop you off. You don't need to be carried into your home, do you?"

"Goodness, no," I protested. "I'm a big girl."

"Are you sure? Do you think you'll be able to walk?"

"Yes, of course. But did you want to come in for tea and cake? You could meet my mother and our peculiar houseguest."

"Thanks, Fina, but I have to get back to work."

I nodded. "Okay, I understand."

The car stopped in front of my house.

I attempted to embrace Aaron goodbye, but it was awkward. His body stiffened. Either he didn't want to hug me or he'd had enough of my hands all over him for one night.

The driver emerged, opened my door, and helped me step out.

I then limped toward the house like a wounded animal.

While opening my gate, the driver circled the cul-de-sac. Then the car paused and Aaron rolled down his window.

"Fina, you forgot your hat."

"Oh, thank you, Aaron," I said as I gratefully accepted it.

"No problem."

I started to turn away when I heard him say,

"I'll call you."

I nodded with surprise, then flew into the house like a bird who'd just escaped Dr. Blackie's claws. I crept upstairs, collapsed into bed, and fell asleep before Mom could interrogate me about the man who had called her.

CHAPTER 12: THE NEXT DAY – MONDAY

I woke with a splitting headache. Mom stood over me while I forced my eyes open.

"Good God," I wailed. "Why is the light so bright?"

"Fina, were you drinking?"

"No."

"Then why were you stumbling across the driveway last night?"

"You saw me?"

"Everyone saw you."

"Who was the man that called asking for your address?"

"A good Samaritan," I joked.

"There's nothing more unattractive than a drunk woman."

I suddenly jolted up. "Did I look that bad?"

"Well…"

"Mom, it was an accident," I exclaimed, jumping out of bed and putting on my robe and slippers. "You know me. I care too much about my figure to drink and add empty calories."

"I know," Mom sighed. "Of course, you still looked beautiful. But it's not like you to get drunk."

"As long as I didn't look foolish in front of Aaron, then who cares. Getting drunk is normal at my age."

"Who is Aaron?"

"Nobody, Mom."

"Okay, Fina, have a good day. I'm off to work."

***

An hour later, I stumbled downstairs and decided to watch *Texas Chain Saw Massacre* to get my mind off last night. I felt like a disaster and knew Beelzebub would feel the same way. Thankfully, Bub only appeared at night when I was awake.

Mom, like a lot of boomers, raised me to be aware of reality. She subjected me to countless war documentaries. I had seen so many Holocaust and Vietnam films by the time I was seven that it almost normalized war and violence.

This made me think of Aaron. What was his childhood like? I needed to know more. Did his father have fits of rage and project them onto his family? Did Aaron suffer? What did he think of war?

I was fascinated by the Japanese occupation of Asia. According to biased accounts, the Japanese saw surrender as grave dishonor and possessed a fight until you die mentality. Did Aaron inherit his grandfather's philosophy?

My encounter with Aaron yesterday had left such a profound impact. The intensity of our encounters on both occasions was so strong that I almost felt feverish. It wasn't just his looks or his presence. There was something subliminal. It was as if he could read my mind. This was highly unusual. Generally, I could quickly get into people's heads while they couldn't reach mine. I sighed, hoping I might hear a voice from one of my former lives suggesting answers. Unfortunately, it had been years since any had whispered a word. Was it because I'd lost my demon powers? Or because I was so focused on my current life? The alcohol from last night certainly didn't help.

Lost in thought, I failed to see the remote control hidden behind the plant. Where did it go? I was impatient, so I switched off the TV by pulling the plug out of the socket. But I yanked the cord too hard, causing an electrical burst. I wondered if I'd broken the wires.

I shrugged and went back upstairs to check my email. I opened my account, hoping to see a message from Jess. But there was nothing. I then checked my phone for texts. Didn't Aaron say he'd call? Didn't he care about my condition, or was he being polite?

I needed to work out. So I tossed my exercise clothes into a gym bag and headed to my fitness club, Clark Hatch. It was where Jess, Selina, Evelina and I used to hang out.

While strolling out of the compound, I wondered where Herman was. I should have asked Mom, but at the time, I honestly didn't care. I was thrilled to have him out of my hair. He was probably off scrounging for pot. Maybe he'd wandered over to Khao San Road, a popular locale for tourists. I hoped he'd stay there forever.

Distracted I failed to notice my neighbor's dogs. Airport and Airplane were the biggest dalmatians I'd ever seen. They lived in a mansion a few blocks over from our modest townhouse. The dogs were yelping and bouncing loudly. Abruptly, I heard a loud, crunching sound. It was a chomping noise. Someone had bitten my buttock.

I screamed, "Oh, my God."

The dogs ran away.

The maids started laughing hysterically. Everyone who had witnessed was pointing and gaping. Pain gripped me. I was certain that my derriere was a bloody mess. Thank God for my thick granny panties—ones Evelina constantly ridiculed. Otherwise, my butt would be toast.

I winced to hold back tears but tossed my head in the air and sauntered off like I was on a catwalk and couldn't care less about the attack. I should have returned home, but instead I hobbled to the top of the street. Then I caught a bus and walked a mile to get to Clark Hatch.

By the time I arrived, I was in agony. Luckily, my favorite fitness instructor, Khun Choke, was more than happy to assist me. After fixing my wounds with antiseptic from the club's medical box, I changed and wandered into the weight room.

I asked Khun Choke, "Have you seen Jess?"

He replied, "Not in months."

Selina texted me: *Fina, we can't work out now. Just woke up. Let's meet at The Bamboo Hut at 3 pm for cake.*

Just woke up? I wondered. It seemed the girls also had a rough night. They didn't invite me? Oh, well. I was too busy fraternizing with my enemy.

When I finished working out, I wandered around the empty gym before heading to the shower. I felt nostalgic remembering all the times I had spent with Jess, Selina, and Evelina. Now it was all over because soon I'd return to the U.S. permanently.

***

I emerged from Clark Hatch feeling energized and had almost forgotten the dog bite. At The Bamboo Hut, the summer air smelled warm and sweet. A ladybug crawled across my arm while sparrows hunted for crumbs.

Selina and Evelina nibbled strawberry short-cake while I sipped a banana smoothie.

I asked, "Girls, have either of you seen or heard from Jess?"

Selina shook her head.

Evelina joked. "Maybe his girlfriend killed him."

"The guy is such a player," Selina explained.

"Sure, but he was a friend, and it seems like he's disappeared from Earth."

"Maybe Jess is with some girl in Pattaya," Evelina suggested.

I sighed. "This missing person case is like Jim Thompson."

"The famous silk entrepreneur?" asked Selina.

"Yes, and allegedly CIA."

Evelina rolled her eyes. "No, it's not. Jess is not that special. Fina, you have a wild imagination."

"Thank you."

"Jess will pop up eventually," Selina assured me.

"Okay," I said hopefully. "Changing the subject, I think my modeling career is over."

"Yes, of course. Modeling is dead now," Selina explained.

"You've always known that," Evelina stated. "Unless you're an actress like me or a pop singer like Selina, then you can't depend on modeling alone."

"You should have entered a beauty pageant. Winners are guaranteed modeling jobs for life," Selina finished.

"You know me," I explained. "I don't love public speaking. Modeling is silent acting."

"Yes, you've always been so shy," Selina agreed.

"Plus, I feel like there's so much I need to read and study."

Selina shook her head. "By then you'll be too old."

Evelina agreed. "Fina, you shouldn't have gone to college."

"Really?"

"In the last two years, you could have gotten so many modeling jobs," Evelina explained.

"I didn't think I'd change that much," I replied.

Evelina crossed her arms. "But you did."

"We grow up so fast," Selina added. "I have an idea."

"You do?"

"Fina, you know that the Thai movie industry is gay," she continued.

"Sure."

"So, you can't sleep with anyone here to get the jobs."

"What are you saying?"

"Go to Hollywood, sleep with someone, and get the roles."

"Sounds like a plan," I joked.

"Of course, you know we'd never do that," Selina insisted.

"Because everyone we know is gay," Evelina finished.

"Thanks for the career advice."

***

I heard Mom return from work, so I crawled out of my cave and stumbled downstairs into the living room.

Mom fiddled with the remote control. "Darn, the TV is out," she complained.

I froze. I immediately realized that I was the guilty party. I was about to exclaim, "It wasn't me" but I caught myself.

Denying my crime might seem overly defensive to Mom. Blaming Herman was tempting. But so far that hadn't worked.

Instead, I placed my hands on my hips and declared, "Ahem?"

"What, Fina?"

"Why do you need TV when you have me?"

Mom shook her head. "I need a different kind of drama. Work has been horrible."

I sat down beside her and pretended to care. "How so?"

"Oh, it's the managing director. He's having

an affair with some bimbo. Now she's on the board of directors. She knows nothing about business and doesn't make good decisions."

"Like what?"

"She wants to fire most of my staff and replace them with her relatives."

"Sounds illegal."

"Yeah, it should be," Mom insisted.

Suddenly she started weeping, which surprised me. Mom rarely cried.

I immediately hugged her. "Is there something else? You're used to nefarious business practices."

"Oh, Fina. I didn't want to tell you."

My stomach dropped. "Tell me what?"

"I quit my job today."

"Quit your job? Oh, my God."

Mom quivered. "Yeah, things are bad. We'll probably lose this house. Your Dad might lose his factories."

"And Khun Jai?"

"We'll have to let her go."

"I'm so sorry, Mom."

"Fina, this isn't your fault."

"If only I'd gotten that shampoo commercial."

"But, you got other jobs."

I stood up. "I didn't make that much, especially since some clients didn't pay."

"I'll find another job," Mom insisted.

I nodded. "I know you will."

"I made lunch reservations for the five of us Thursday at Pan Pan."

"The five of us?"

"Yes, you, me, Herman, Tom, and Roxanne."

"Ah, okay," I said without much enthusiasm.

I hugged Mom, swiped a banana from the center-piece, and headed back to my room. I was scared. With Mom unemployed, I'd have to get a full-time job to cover expenses. I could barely pay bills while working part-time and going to school.

Instantly, I missed Hell because I felt stressed and helpless. I crawled into bed and hugged my pillow. I thought about Aaron and how he'd said, "Oh, baby, you're so cuddly." Was this his standard line? It was a strange line and didn't match him. Or did Aaron only say it to me because he thinks I'm chubby?

I also thought about his promise to call me. He hadn't. Didn't he wonder if I'd recover? Surely he'd seen me hobbling like a wounded cat. Was Aaron just another player? I rolled around, tensing my body, and clenching my teeth as I overanalyzed the endless possibilities. The more I agonized, the more wound up I became. Finally, I drifted to sleep.

CHAPTER 13: THURSDAY – THREE DAYS LATER

Lunch

It was close to noon, so Herman and I met Mom at Pan Pan —— a trendy Italian restaurant and personal family favorite. Generally, I didn't eat pasta or pizza, but since my modeling career was over, I would.

I wasn't excited to see Mom's friend Tom Barger, a silver-haired, blue-eyed scoundrel.

Flashback

When I was fourteen, I went with Mom to her friend Janet's house for poker night. As we arrived, I squealed and jumped in the air to evade a flying cock-

roach. Mom grabbed me by the arm. "Fina, don't act like that." I quivered. "I'm scared. I hate insects."

Mom whispered in my ear, "Janet is a strong woman. She hates girly girls, so don't act like that."

Strong woman? *I wondered.* She's aggressive and not always kind, but apparently strength and character are not measured by how caring we are. *Society's standards infuriated me.*

I swallowed hard as Janet approached. Her beady eyes scrutinized me. Then she quipped, "Fina, your lipstick doesn't match your outfit."

"Thanks for letting me know," I replied sincerely while she barged out to the parking lot to see Tom.

Mom clasped my elbow. "What an awful thing to say."

"What?"

"Janet's remark about your lipstick."

I shrugged. "She's always like that. Why are you friends with her?"

Mom became impatient. "Janet has been very good to me."

"But she hates me?"

Mom smiled. "Janet hates pretty girls. So do a lot of women. So be careful about how you act, Fina."

"Mom, there are so many sweet ladies you could be friends with..."

"Fina, stop it. Don't criticize my friends. They are intellectuals."

I said nothing while walking into Janet's house. I sat down in the living room and began reading Jane

Eyre *for fun.*

When Tom entered, he made a beeline for me and pinched my right arm.

"Hey!" I snapped.

"What's that?" Tom asked, pointing to a gold box on my lap.

"A gift from a classmate," I replied. I had come straight to poker night from school.

"An admirer?"

"Yes."

Tom's eyes twinkled. "Godiva chocolates?"

"Would you like them?" I asked.

"No, but lay off the sweets, Fina—otherwise, you'll get fat."

I was livid and about to tell Tom to buzz off, but then his twenty-something Thai wife walked in. She was at least half his age. I felt sorry for her because she was sweet.

Mom laughed. "Oh, Fina, you know Tom. He loves to tease you. Calm down, honey. Don't be so sensitive."

"Oh, Marie, you mustn't let Fina read those romances. They'll mess with her head," Tom opined.

Mom sighed. "I know, Tom. I wish she'd read more stuff from the '70s as we do."

***

Today we were meeting Tom and his daughter. Roxanne was over thirty and lived in New York. She had short-brown hair and a petite but stocky build. Tom and Roxanne sat at a corner table.

After brief introductions, I sat next to Roxanne. She turned to me and asked, "What will you do after graduation?"

"Gosh, I've no idea," I replied.

Roxanne smiled. "What's your major?"

"Political Science."

"Ha, ha. That'll be useful," Roxanne joked. "Maybe polish it off with a minor in poetry."

Herman snorted.

Tom piped in, "Yeah, Fina. Good luck getting a job with that degree."

I was thankful when the waitress came to take orders.

After she left, Mom declared, "Fina will go to law school."

Really?" Roxanne asked suspiciously. "Why?"

"I'm descended from a long line of thieves. Therefore, I'll follow family tradition," I joked.

Mom choked on her breadstick while exclaiming, "Fina, you're most certainly not descended from criminals."

"Define criminal," I said, dryly.

Tom smirked.

Mom shook her head. "Fina, you're unbelievable."

I exhaled. "Lawyers rise high in prisons."

"What?" Mom demanded.

Herman nodded. "She's right, Marie. Lawyers do well in prison."

"You're planning to end up in prison?" Roxanne asked.

"Very ambitious," Tom remarked sarcastically.

Mom looked impatient. "Fina wants to work for the State Department."

"I do?" I asked.

"Yeah, you're quite the diplomat," Herman said in a snarky tone.

I tossed my hair back and bragged. "When I was four, Mom had me play with little boys whose dads worked at the Embassy. Jake was a bully. So, one day after I'd had enough, I picked up a chair and was about to crush Jake's skull. Unfortunately, Mom intervened."

I was throwing subtle hints at Tom and Herman. Unfortunately, both were too dense to pick up on my repressed desires. Evidently, my demon nature lingered even after three years of being entirely human. This made sense. It would be impossible to quash billions of years of history immediately.

Tom nodded. "Fina, you were born a diplomat. If you don't get your way, use force."

I smiled while Herman whined, "Yeah, like with me."

Roxanne smiled at my enemy. "Fina bullies you?"

The waitress placed pizza and salad on the red checkered table cloth.

"Shouldn't we eat?" I suggested.

Herman caught Roxanne's gaze and replied, "Like you wouldn't believe."

Tom nodded. "Hey, buddy. We've all been there."

"Good God, what is this?" I demanded.

"An intervention," Mom clarified.

I heard my cell ring, dropped my slice of pizza, and explained, "I've got to take this."

I rushed outside and was thrilled to hear my agent's voice.

"Khun Jin? What's up?"

"Fina, can you come to the agency now?"

"Sure, what for?"

"A casting. Please come quickly."

I rushed back to the table. "Sorry, guys, I have to run. I've got a casting."

***

When I arrived at the agency, I rushed in like it was my first casting. Or maybe deep down I figured it might be my last. Khun Jin and other bookers were on the phone. I sat on a sofa in the waiting room and rifled through *Vogue*. Selina was on the cover of a local edition. Inside, she promoted her singing career as the industry's pop princess.

Finally, Khun Jin emerged from her office. Before she could speak, I blurted, "Wow, so I'm back in the game?"

My agent thought for a moment. "Some clients will be here soon."

"I came over so fast that I didn't have time to go home to get my portfolio."

Khun Jin nodded. "It's okay, Fina."

"I guess we can just show them my comp cards," I babbled nervously. Something didn't feel right. I sensed tension.

My agent sat down next to me. "This casting is for the role of a mommy."

"What?" I stuttered. "I'm only twenty-one. I'm too young."

"Twenty-one is old enough to have children."

"I guess." I crossed my arms and pouted.

"Fina, your look is very mature. You're too old for cosmetics. Fresh-faced thirteen-year-olds seize those roles."

I sighed. "What's the product? Does it pay well?"

"Milk powder. The pay is okay. This TVC is for China."

I nodded. "They don't care about my recent scandal?"

Khun Jin's mouth tightened. "Since the clients are from China, they don't watch the local news. I don't think they know about the cake incident."

"That's a relief."

"They saw your pictures and think you're perfect for playing a Mommy."

There was a knock at the door. A group of Chinese clients walked in. We all headed to the boardroom.

While sitting down, an older man exclaimed, "You look familiar."

"You probably recognize me from my comp card?"

He glanced at my cards and shook his head. "Nah, you don't look like your headshot."

A worried expression grew across my face. "I don't?"

"When were these taken?"

"Last year," Khun Jin interjected. She was lying. The photos were four years old.

The client eyed me knowingly. "You like gambling?"

Silence filled the air. My agent glared at me.

Finally, I exclaimed, "Good heavens, no!"

"I saw you at The Hibiscus a few weeks ago. You were playing poker with a guy named Walker."

"You know Aaron?" I asked. Instantly, I forgot about my casting and was intrigued.

"Yeah, I often see him in Macao."

"What can you tell me about him?"

The client glared at me. "Why?"

"Just curious."

"So, it's true."

I exclaimed, "Wait. Please let me explain."

It was too late. The clients had already stood up. They were impatient and began leaving. It was apparent this part wouldn't be mine.

Khun Jin eyed me like a disappointed parent.

I was determined to clear my reputation, so I ran out to the waiting room and stammered, "I wasn't playing poker."

The clients stopped. The fat man looked at me. "Don't lie. Everyone saw you playing poker with Walker. You even went to the terrace alone with him."

"It's not what it looked like."

"The following Sunday, I saw you on his riverboat. You were so drunk you could barely stand. Walker carried you into his car."

Khun Jin looked utterly disgusted. The rest of the office had gathered to watch the confrontation.

The client shook his finger at me. "In China, a good Mommy doesn't drink and act like a sailor."

I swallowed. "Okay, well, maybe that's not how things are done in China. But I'm American, so I call my shenanigans—American mommy-style."

The clients and Khun Jin stared with stoic expressions. An awkward silence grew.

Tony, a blonde male model, approached. With his thick Texan accent, he piped in, "That's not American mommy-style. At least not where I grew up."

I exhaled. "Who cares? What I do—when, where, and how—is my business and mine alone. I don't want Mommy roles anyway."

I then pivoted and stormed out of the office. I'd had it. I was sick of being judged. I ran down the five flights of stairs as fast as I could.

While marching through the narrow streets to find a taxi, I thought about my modeling career. Only yesterday, I'd been a fourteen-year-old filled with hope.

When my first agent met me, she was breathless and said to Mom, "Marie, thank you so much for bringing Fina to me." Then she leaned down and whispered in my ear, "Honey, you're going to make me a lot of money."

A few days later, I went to a James-Bond themed whiskey casting where the directors snapped pictures and wrote *Age 21* on the back of my images. I was almost cast as the Bond girl, but then Kitty and I were walking down a back alley. I tripped over a pothole and got hit by a motorcycle. I wasn't hurt, but the bruises took weeks to heal.

Everyone scolded me for being a klutz, but I was only fourteen. My behavior fit my age. Now, I was twenty-one and perfect for whiskey ads. Instead, I was once again scolded for acting my age.

CHAPTER 14:
A FEW HOURS
LATER

When I arrived home, Roxanne, Mom, and Herman were watching a movie.

While entering, I asked, "Is that *Return to Paradise* with Vince Vaughn?"

Roxanne looked up with a sleepy smile. "Yes, isn't Vaughn dreamy?"

I paused for a moment. "I guess."

Herman rolled his eyes. "What's with women and Vince Vaughn? In New York, he's just an average Joe."

"Isn't this film about petty drug dealers? Right up your alley, isn't it, Herman?"

"Hey!" he snapped.

"Guys, cut it out. We're trying to watch the film," Mom ordered while tossing popcorn into her mouth.

***

I bounced upstairs to my bedroom and began bolting the door. Abruptly, it swung wide open, and a heavy breeze blew through my hair. A shadow lurked on my balcony.

"Beelzebub," I gasped. I'd completely forgotten about him. It was barely dark. I wasn't expecting to see him, at least not this early in the evening.

His red eyes bulged while glaring at me. The vein in his neck protruded.

I threw my purse on the floor and sat in my white rattan peacock chair. Beelzebub sat down on my white lace comforter.

Neither said anything.

Tension grew.

Finally, I broke the silence by stammering, "I can explain—"

Beelzebub rolled his eyes, then snapped, "Save it. No one wants your explanations."

"But, but—"

"You know what your problem is, Fina?"

"I'm too intelligent?"

"No! You're always trying to explain yourself."

"A well-developed argument requires an in-depth analysis."

Beelzebub shook his head with disgust. "Henry James said, 'a lady should never have to explain herself.'"

"Apparently, I'm not much of a lady," I replied contritely.

"By whose standards?"

"My agent and various clients."

"Why would you care what any of these people think?"

"Some of us need to work. I need money."

"Have you forgotten your mission to take out Walker?"

"Not entirely."

"Not entirely?"

"Look, a lot is going on in my life. Mom quit her job, and Dad's on the verge of his second bankruptcy. I have two years of college left. Then I need to get a real job."

"Please stop. Just stop it with the excuses."

I sighed. "The problem with Aaron is I'm not sure he matters."

"Ha," Beelzebub quipped, with a sly grin.

"What?"

"I think someone has a crush." He waved his finger at me playfully.

"I most certainly do not," I protested. "It's just that Aaron's father doesn't seem very important. Even if his Dad *did* train the men who tortured and killed those students, he was just following orders. We should focus on the men in charge—at the very top."

"Can't, they're either dead or untouchable."

"Maybe Aaron and his father have suffered enough."

"Oh?" Beelzebub's countenance was quizzical.

I stammered, "It's like that book—*Ordinary Men*, by Christopher Browning. Regular men were forced to carry out orders they didn't agree with. It hurt them terribly."

"Apologist propaganda," Beelzebub retorted dryly.

I shook my head. "Many can't live with themselves."

"Don't get soft, Fina. Aaron's father was a career soldier. He joined because he *enjoyed* killing."

I exhaled. "Alright, when Aaron calls me again, I'll meet him one more time."

"Calls you? You're awfully confident."

"Please have some patience."

"Fina, unlike you, I have all the time in the world." Beelzebub then stepped onto my balcony, jumped off, and flew away.

I took a deep breath and thought, *Such a typical demon*. But my concern was interrupted by a heavy knock at my door.

"Yes?" I asked.

"Fina, it's Mom. I have a present for you."

I opened the door. "A gift? Why?"

"You know me. I just like to buy things when I see something unique."

This was so my mother. It's also why we were always broke.

Mom entered and sat down on my bed with a shopping bag.

Anxiously, I opened it and exclaimed, "Designer hip-hop gear?"

"Yes. After twelve years of ballet, you should be able to dance hip-hop."

I crossed my arms. "God, I wish. Mom, is it okay if I give the pants to Selina?"

"Why? Why don't you like them?"

I sighed. "I never wear these types of pants, but Selina does."

"Call Selina. We can all meet at Scarlet Sugar in an hour?"

"Are you serious?"

"Yeah! Let's go out for drinks and dancing."

I sighed. "Sure. I'll call Selina and Evelina."

***

Herman, Roxanne, Mom, and I had been at Scarlet Sugar since 9:30 p.m. It was a popular sports bar catering to ex-pats. The room was expansive with wooden floors and red lighting that cast a ruby glow. A band would soon play.

Mom and Herman were at a table in the corner. A waitress took their order for Margaritas, onion rings, and French fries. Roxanne and I went to the bar to order wine. It was an excuse to chat with patrons.

Instantly, a well-built guy in a suit approached me and asked, "Where are you from?"

I swallowed and started to explain, "Mom's from Minnesota, but—"

The guy joked, "I hate people from the Midwest."

"I'm sure everyone must love you," I said dryly. I moved over so Roxanne could stand between us.

"Hey, so did you want to join me on my yacht tomorrow?" the guy continued.

I ignored him and retreated. I slid into a table next to Mom. Roxanne followed with our drinks and took a chair opposite.

"Fina, are you insane?" Roxanne whispered. "That guy was so hot."

"Yeah, I'm the crazy one," I replied sarcastically.

"So many women in New York would fight over him."

"Deaf women?" I joked.

"He looks like a dick," Herman interjected.

For once, Herman had something useful to say.

I checked my phone, wondering where Selina and Evelina were.

Suddenly they both appeared. Both said hello to Mom.

I introduced Selina and Evelina to Herman and Roxanne. Neither was impressed with Herman, whose vacant look was even more apparent tonight.

"Selina, I thought you might like these," I said, handing her a shopping bag.

She clasped the bag, opened it, and removed the pants. "Fina, these are so me."

"I thought so."

"Hold on while I change into them." Selina took off for the ladies' room.

"Okay, girls, I want to see some dancing," Mom ordered. "Fina, let's see the results of your ballet lessons."

I sighed. Selina was a professional hip-hop teacher, so she led the way to the dance floor. Roxanne and Evelina followed. Herman, being the lethargic creature he was, stayed with Mom at the table.

The four of us started dancing. The band was playing The Killers' *Mr. Brightside*. Selina pulled me to the center and tried unsuccessfully to show me her moves. Meanwhile, Roxanne was completely sloshed and very into the music. Evelina stood back and watched us with narrowed eyes and crossed arms. She was judging us.

During mid-show, the singer spotted us. It wasn't difficult since we were the only four on the floor. However, there were plenty of people clustered at the bar. The singer jumped off the stage and inched his way toward Roxanne. He put his arm around her and said, "Baby, you're my ballerina." She giggled.

Roxanne wasn't built like a ballerina. She joked about rarely hitting the gym and subsisting on a diet of junk food and beer.

The performer worked his way over to me and Selina, whom he admired fondly. However, he then turned to me. With a menacing glare, he bellowed loudly on the microphone, "But, you... you dance like a buffalo on ice-skates."

No one laughed. I quickly backed away.

"Get the Hell out of here!" screamed the singer.

"Gladly," I responded, and we all left the club.

Once outside, Mom asked, "Is that guy clinical?"

"What a weird guy," Evelina agreed. She was loyal. It was one thing for her to give me a hard time, but quite another for a stranger to, let alone a man.

No one else said anything.

Roxanne beamed. "I think he liked me because I move to the music. I feel the rhythm."

Herman smiled at her.

"Did I look that bad?" I asked.

Selina wrapped her arm around me. "You've had too much ballet, Fina."

I laughed. "Is there such a thing?"

Selina continued, "The problem is that you're 100% girl."

"Yes, that is a problem," I agreed.

She finished, "Street requires—"

"Confidence," Roxanne interjected.

"Yeah," Evelina agreed.

I sighed. "Thanks, guys."

Roxanne continued, "Fina, at first you had it —you were dancing great. But then suddenly you looked insecure."

"So, that made it okay?" I asked.

"I didn't say that," Roxanne replied. "I'm explaining why you got attacked."

While talking, I didn't notice Aaron and his friends approaching. They were trying to brush past us to enter Scarlett Sugar.

Aaron grinned when he saw me. "Fina."

"Oh, hey, what a surprise," I replied, a bit startled.

"Yeah. Sorry I didn't call."

"Aaron, let me introduce you to my friends and Mom."

While making introductions, Aaron beamed. He asked me, "Do you want to join us?"

"Thank you, but I have to go."

Aaron nodded, waved goodbye to us, and took off with his friends.

Roxanne watched Aaron leave. "Who was that guy? Did you see his arms? Wow!"

Evelina and Selina shrugged. They were used to athletic male models.

Herman whined, "The guy looks like a creeper."

Mom waved her hand to hail a taxi. "I think it's time to go home."

I broke away and started walking rapidly in

the opposite direction.

"I need to be alone," I explained. "I'll see you later."

I passed stalls selling Buddhist handicrafts and handwoven garments. Beyonce and Lady Gaga blasted loudly through the streets. Bangkok was wide awake—bright lights glittered for miles. Tuk-tuks and taxis plowed through the soot-covered streets. Vendors hawked coconut cakes and banana pastries while a rat crawled onto the sidewalk.

I heard Selina shout, "Fina, wait up."

I stopped and spun around.

"Fina, let's go to the Lemon Drop," Evelina suggested.

"Okay," I agreed. The three of us strolled over to the popular hangout.

The Lemon Drop was an ultra-modern club distinguished by disco lighting, yellow décor, and a maze of mirrors. We sat at a high-top table in a corner. While ordering Lemontinis, I got a text.

Hey, where are you? It was from Aaron.

I didn't respond.

"Someone texting you?" Selina asked.

I nodded. "Yeah, that guy."

"The one with the tattoos?" Evelina asked with an arched eyebrow. "He's not exactly your type."

Selina shrugged. "So what? Fina, ask him to join."

"Are you sure?" I asked.

"Yes! Call him," Evelina insisted.

I texted back: *We're at the Lemon Drop.*

Aaron immediately texted back: *Cool, I'll be right over.*

***

Aaron appeared with his friends, who quickly engaged with Selina and Evelina. The Lemon Drop quickly packed. The increased volume made it impossible to talk.

Aaron whispered into my ear. "Hey, do you want to get out of here?"

"Sure," I agreed.

Aaron's eyes flickered with excitement.

"Can we go to Starbucks across the street?"

"I guess," Aaron replied.

I explained to Evelina and Selina that Aaron and I were going across the street. They nodded supportively and moved on to the dance floor with Aaron's friends.

Upon exiting, a warm breeze blew through my hair. The air smelled of heat and cigarette smoke. We sauntered across the street. Aaron's steps were steady. Neither of us said anything. I observed a cluster of girls approaching. They were very slim, dark-skinned, and wore short skirts. I sighed and wondered if they wanted to proposition Aaron.

Much to my surprise, they echoed excitedly, "Fina!"

"Me?" I asked, pointing a finger to my chest.

The girls nodded while pulling out notepads and pens. "Can you please sign your autograph?"

While I signed my name, the women asked, "Fina, we didn't see you in television commercials for a while. Where did you go?"

"I've been studying in the U.S."

They smiled, thanked me, and quickly moved back to their corner outside of a bar catering to ex-pat men.

I exhaled, thinking, *The most vulnerable members of society have always been here, supporting and comforting me. What have I ever done for them?*

Waves of guilt overwhelmed me.

What was my problem? I had the opportunity to get an education and make a better life for myself. These women did not. They were likely the daughters of farmers unable to pay off debts. The IMF loans sold to Thailand had placed a considerable burden on the poor who had trouble paying high VAT taxes.

My popularity had always been strong in rural areas. For example, one day Kitty trekked through the jungle with friends. They stopped at the hut of a guerilla leader. When Kitty entered his home, she was startled to see one of my cosmetics ads hanging on the wall. Kitty was not happy and complained, "Thousands of miles from home, and I still can't escape Fina."

Why did I need to return to Hell? I was already there. If I wanted to help those who'd helped me all my life and supported me when I was down, I needed to get my act together.

"Fina, do you want to try this place?" Aaron suggested.

Lost in thought, I'd almost forgotten him. "Sure."

We entered a moody coffee bar, The Pink Lotus.

Aaron chose a wooden table in a corner.

"I'll take the chair," I insisted.

"Okay."

"In my family, it's customary for the men to sit facing the entrance."

"Really?" Aaron asked with a smile.

I nodded. "That way, you can draw your sword."

Aaron raised an eyebrow. "Raise my sword?"

I nodded. "It's an Ancient Chinese military tradition."

We sat under a Casablanca fan. It blew unused napkins off tables and onto the black and white tile floors.

We studied the menus. A waitress approached.

"Do you have fruit?" I asked.

"Only bananas," she replied.

"Banana is a fruit," Aaron explained with a big grin.

"I'll have orange juice."

Aaron ordered a black coffee. He leaned back and smiled. There was an awkward silence.

I stammered, "Gosh, about the other night."

Aaron smirked while his eyes narrowed. I blinked rapidly.

"I was very drunk. I never drink."

His smile vanished. "You mentioned that."

I protested, "I don't normally create such a scene."

He chuckled, leaned back, and steepled his hands. "Are you religious?"

Rarely did anyone ask this question. "Maybe, sort of."

Aaron stared.

I continued, "Not exactly."

Aaron smiled. "I was raised strict Catholic."

"I'm sorry to hear that," I remarked dryly.

"Oh?"

"I just remembered that I'm Protestant."

Aaron crossed his arms. "You just remembered?"

"My mother was raised to be a nun."

"Really?" His eyes widened.

"Yes, in my family, the worst thing you can be is Protestant."

"You just said that you're Protestant."

"Exactly." I leaned forward. "My great-grandfather was Scottish. He pursued my great-grandmother for fifteen years. She refused to marry him because he wasn't Catholic."

There was amusement in Aaron's eyes. Was it my passion or story that made him chuckle?

I continued, "I can't imagine anything so overbearing."

"What?"

"Forcing someone to change religions. I'm opposed to interventionism. The sixteenth century interests me because it was an era of religious wars."

Aaron sipped his coffee. "Interesting."

"I'm not fond of hierarchy."

"Is this a conversation we should have here?"

"You don't like politics?"

"Not really."

I narrowed my eyes. "Why?"

"People get angry."

"You fear confrontation?"

Aaron shrugged. "Had too much of it."

"Life is conflict."

Aaron crossed his arms. "Is there a lot of conflict in your life?"

"Nothing atypical for my age."

"You seem mature for your age."

I smiled. "I bet you say that to lots of women."

Aaron's smile vanished, and his countenance tensed. "No, never." I'd expected him to joke *but with you, I meant it*, as he had the other night.

I nodded. "I guess."

"How old are you?"

"Twenty-one."

"Seems like you've never been a child."

I bit my lip angrily. "I've heard that before."

"Sorry, I didn't mean to upset you."

I sipped my juice. "It's okay."

Aaron teased, "So, what's your mission?"

My body stiffened. "What are you talking about." Did Aaron know I was hunting him? It's like he already knew me so well.

He tilted his head. "You said your great-grandmother converted your-great grandfather."

I blinked rapidly and touched my neck. "I don't have a mission. I'm not on any crusade like my ancestors, who invaded the Muslim world. I don't believe in changing people. I support peoples' rights of self-determination."

"Like Vietnam?"

"Exactly. Sovereign nations have the right to independence."

"Sure, but what if those governments are oppressing individual rights?"

I swallowed. "All for the greater good, right?"

Aaron shook his head. "I disagree."

I looked down. "I guess I'm still trying to figure this out."

"You care about the Natives, don't you?"

I bit my lip and looked into Aaron's eyes. "Sure."

"Why?"

I glanced out the window. Coffee-skinned

children wearing rags played in the streets.

"We never forget who we cared about when we were young, right?"

Aaron sipped his coffee. "Maybe."

"My father's family is icy and formal. We don't hug."

"Sure."

"When I was eleven, I fell off a boat. A group of sea gypsies fished me out and carried me to shore. They saved me."

Aaron listened but said nothing. Once again, I had this eerie feeling that he knew far more about me than he let on. I blinked nervously, which only added to his amusement. It occurred to me that Aaron might know more about me than I knew about myself, which gave him the power that I generally possessed. Panic spread throughout my limbs. It was clear I was in a weaker position, and I was not too fond of it.

I felt embarrassed talking so much and over-sharing. I decided to change the subject. "Gosh, Aaron, your accent isn't Midwestern, and it isn't Texan."

Aaron smiled broadly, leaned forward, and explained, "English wasn't my first language."

"I'm always envious of people who grew up in a bilingual home."

"Didn't you?"

I shook my head. "I learned English from Mom."

Aaron nodded. "Yeah, I was noticing your accent."

"It used to be Midwestern, but now it's very —"

Aaron grinned. "International."

"Thank you," I replied, but I was bored with our conversation. It felt shallow and insipid.

Aaron didn't say much. Once again, I had to ask questions. "Do you miss home?"

His eyes lit up. It's like he came alive whenever I asked questions. "Not really. People back home are so boring and not ambitious."

"I understand."

"I go home, and my classmates are bartending."

"At least they work," I joked.

"Oh, yeah?"

"I know plenty of glorified bums."

Aaron's eyes instantly grew severe. "The leisure classes?"

"Sure."

"Yeah, but all those connections—"

This line of discussion always made me uncomfortable. Instinctively, I wanted to bolt, so I pulled out my wallet. Aaron shook his head and insisted on paying.

"Thank you," I repeated.

"For business, relationships matter," Aaron explained.

I looked at my watch. "Oh, my God, Aaron, I

have to go. It's late, and Mom will be worried."

His smile vanished.

"Thank you for the juice," I nervously repeated.

I jumped up and rushed to the door, but when I tried to open it, I couldn't. The glass door was so heavy.

Aaron stood up. "Hey, let me get that for you." With ease, he pulled the door open.

I gave him a radiant smile. "Goodbye."

Aaron didn't smile. His brows furrowed, and he clenched his jaw while watching me fly out of the Pink Lotus. I hadn't forgotten my plan to murder Aaron, but I no longer cared. He didn't seem worth the bother. I had more important goals.

CHAPTER 15: WEDNESDAY

The next day, I accidentally slept until noon. By the time I rolled out of bed and stumbled into the living room, everyone was out. I was thankful to have some time alone because Mom, Herman, and Roxanne were getting on my nerves.

Dr. Blackie sat on the dining room table. My ally looked at me with his yellow eyes and white eyelashes.

I reached out to pet him. "Hey, little buddy. You don't like Herman either?"

"*Meow*."

"Yeah, he's a creep." I picked up my cat and stroked his silky tuxedo. "We've been together a long time, haven't we?"

"*Meow*."

I gently set Blackie down and raced back upstairs. I quickly dressed and packed a gym bag for Clark Hatch. But instead of heading to my usual hangout, I trekked to the Hilton downtown near the British Embassy.

The Hilton possessed a luxurious interior beset with high-vault ceilings, marble floors, teak paneling, and Thai silk seating. The hotel smelled of chilled jasmine while tropical trees hid its outdoor swimming pool.

I sauntered to the fitness center. The weight and exercise rooms were empty since most members were at work. However, through the glass windows, I observed people playing golf in the distance.

While entering the ladies' room, I texted Mom: *At Hilton.*

Mom: *By the pool?*

Me: *Yep.*

Mom: *Be there soon.*

While slipping into my purple swimsuit, I thought about what I wanted in life.

Ever since my casting disaster, I'd felt different. It was liberating not having a noose around my neck.

Flashback

Since I was fourteen, agents had practically owned me. I'd been exclusive with a top agency during my entire time in high school. After graduation, I took off a year to model, but little changed. I'd held contracts with other agencies in the region: Hong Kong, Taipei, Singapore, and Manila.

When I moved to Eugene, Oregon, I didn't expect

to continue modeling. I popped into an agency in Portland with a portfolio containing mostly tear sheets, which didn't seem like a big deal to me. Selina, Evelina, and some of my Eurasian friends had rooms filled with tear sheets: catalogs, magazines, print ads, and calendars. I had only a trunk and a shelf.

I met with an agency in Portland, where a blonde woman named Karen flipped through my book. She blithely said, "Honey. You're just not the look."

I nodded. "Because I'm Asian?"

"Um, actually, we have an Asian market. The problem is you're not exactly Asian."

"Uh, huh."

Karen pulled out books of her top working girls: blondes. However, their portfolios contained only tests with local photographers. The office was empty. Phones didn't ring as they did at my other agencies.

Karen continued, "Fina, you're so calm."

I smiled but was confused.

She continued, "Our models are much more excited."

I sighed. In big markets, you lose your ego fast because you accept competition and constant rejection. Further, appearing effortless was essential.

"Your pictures are alright..."

I tilted my head but didn't say anything because, at nineteen, I'd learned more in five years of modeling than I would in a lifetime. Karen's responses echoed her business. A few weeks ago, I'd received enthusiasm from MTV Asia and Taiwanese soap operas, where the *market was hungry with excitement. You could feel the energy.*

"Fina, your television commercials are very impressive. You've done a lot of work."

"Yes, and dozens of music videos. I almost starred in Asian films, but my American accent is too thick."

Karen had a short attention span and didn't care. She stood up and walked me to the door.

"Thanks for coming by. If we have anything, we'll call."

A week later, the Portland agency called. Soon, I had catalog jobs, tests with a famous photographer, and appeared on a CD cover. But after I started college, traveling five hours for castings and shoots was exhausting. Besides school, I waited tables. On the weekends, I taught modeling classes at a local talent agency in Eugene. But I was happiest while analyzing history or problem-solving.

***

I exited the ladies' room and waded into the swimming pool. The water shimmered like turquoise, and the air smelled of jasmine. Waiters served piña coladas to European tourists sunbathing while a friendly breeze whipped through my hair.

I swam the breaststroke so I could keep my head above water and avoid getting my hair or face wet. While swimming my first lap, I thought about

Beelzebub's mission. The scent of chlorine was strong. Leaves and ants floated across the surface. A caterpillar inched his way along the edges.

How did I now feel about Hell? Did I genuinely want to return? Hell had been home for billions of years. It offered endless challenge and was therefore exciting. Its inhabitants kept me on my toes. Heaven was pleasant but incredibly stifling. I couldn't breathe under its restraints. For example, there were strict restrictions regarding what one could and couldn't say.

I'd only been on Earth as Fina for twenty-one years. However, I'd inhabited other female forms in different decades and centuries. Unfortunately, I was still struggling to remember their exact identities. I suspected that my strongest former lives were as British women from the Victorian Era, not necessarily English. They might have been Welsh, Scottish, or Irish. But they were level-headed, autonomous, and self-reliant. There were also voices from the Ancient Far East, but they were either excessively pragmatic or more subdued and melancholy. It was tempting to ask Beelzebub, but he'd probably fabricate a story to manipulate me.

Initially, the chaos of Earth got on my nerves. But now it didn't feel very different from Hell. I'd been here long enough to develop a strong sense of self—independent of Satan. What kind of a brother was he? I never heard from him.

Satan insisted on communicating through

Beelzebub, who was a domineering, untrust-worthy control freak. With a mentor like Bub, who needed enemies? I was tired of his snide tone and blatant manipulation. The guy was about as subtle as a blowtorch.

No wonder Beelzebub hated my twin. Satan was callous and a bad brother, but he was smooth. When Satan wanted something done, his charm was so effective it was impossible to see through his machinations. Beelzebub couldn't be trusted. Even if I killed Aaron, would it guarantee my safe return to Hell?

If I knew Bub, this was a trick. I'd kill a use-less person and wind up in prison on Earth for the rest of my mortal years. Then where would I go? Back to Hell? If I went that route, I'd be just another lost soul, which meant an eternity in a forced labor camp. I wouldn't enjoy the status of being Satan's twin: a seat on the Board and work of my choice.

I completed ten laps, climbed out of the pool, and felt shifty eyes upon me. I tiptoed over to a lounge chair and began toweling off. I sat down to check my texts. None were from Aaron.

What did I think of Aaron? Well, I didn't think he was worth killing as I'd argued with Be-elzebub earlier. Aaron's father didn't seem import-ant enough to care about. This assignment was in-sulting. I'd been a recruiter for billions of years, and my task was to influence powerful world leaders—presidents and prime ministers.

I wasn't an assassin. But if I were to kill anyone, I'd start at the top and not the bottom. According to perfunctory research, Aaron's dad joined the Army when he was barely eighteen. So he was a naïve pawn in this Byzantine game of chess.

Did Troy join the military, thinking he was a modern crusader embarking upon a mission to destroy tyranny? Did Troy's intent even matter? Aaron wasn't responsible for anything his father did. If anything, he was a victim. He likely grew up absorbing trauma.

Aaron didn't strike me as evil. Then again, he didn't seem particularly good. Aaron seemed like a very basic, ordinary guy. He liked beer, sports, and women. His line of work was questionable. Then again, who was I to judge?

Initially, Aaron seemed intriguing. However, our recent encounter left much to be desired. It wasn't necessarily anything he did or didn't say. I just picked up on something I didn't like. I had a strong suspicion we'd meet again.

I was reading the drink and snack menu when Mom sidled up. Herman hugged her heels.

"Fina, have you been here long?"

"About an hour."

"You must be hungry. We're starving."

I nodded. "Sure, but traffic is insane."

"Yeah, let's order canapes while we wait for traffic to die down."

After ordering, I started reading *Time*. Across the cover were images of Abu Ghraib. Shocking footage of soldiers beating detainees at Abu Ghraib prison in Iraq had gripped the world.

An overweight tourist in a Speedo slithered up. He had a round face, big nose, and beady eyes. "Whoa, a beautiful woman who reads," he joked.

I nodded politely. "*Time* is kind of mainstream, but it was the only newsworthy publication in the ladies' room."

"You're smart," the guy continued.

And you're condescending, I thought.

"Fina's not into politics," Mom interjected. "But I am."

Just because I dislike arguing with strangers doesn't mean I'm not abreast of current affairs, I thought bitterly.

"Oh, yeah," asked the stranger. He had a strong New York accent and didn't look as excited to talk to Mom.

"My name's Marie, and I'm a leftist." This was routine. My mother was extroverted and loved chatting with random people.

Over the years, Mom didn't attend many photo shoots, but when she did, she managed to share all of her political views. She was not a mysterious woman, so I stopped taking her to shoots, which suited her. My family dismissed the entertainment industry as shallow and vapid. I was used to this narrow-minded approach, especially from high-brow Marxists.

In fact, most industry-professionals were artists who'd devoted years of training to their craft. I'd learned a lot about business from modeling: communication, analyzing contracts, sales, marketing, and negotiations.

It was through modeling that I met other Eurasians. They were my competition, but we rarely remembered this while sharing stories. I worked well with models from the former Soviet Republics. We bonded over our communist upbringings and fervent desires to forge ahead as entrepreneurs in free markets. Thus, if pseudo-intellectuals felt superior looking down on us, well, their scorn was to their detriment.

Herman observed us while cramming his face with French fries. He occasionally paused to roll his eyes.

"What do you think of Abu Ghraib?" Mom asked.

The stranger's eyes widened. "Truly sickening. The perps should be punished."

"Starting at the top," Mom countered.

I left to shower and change while Mom continued her lively discussion. I could always count on her to trust the oddest people. Last summer, I got a call:

Flashback

Guy: Hey, are you Fina?

Me: Maybe.

Guy: Fina, I met your mom at the Foreign Correspondence Club in Bangkok.

Me: Oh, cool.

Guy: Yeah, I'm in Eugene right now.

Me: And she suggested you call me?

Guy: Yeah, she said you're a model. Are you?

Me: Sorry, I have to go.

Who needs problems when you have family?

CHAPTER 16: AN HOUR LATER

We met Roxanne for dinner at The Sweet Salsa, a trendy Mexican restaurant downtown.

"Mom, I think this place is way out of budget."

"Oh, really?" Roxanne asked.

"Mom quit her job," I explained.

"I'm sorry to hear that," Roxanne said genuinely.

Herman didn't say anything because he was too focused on cramming chips into his mouth. Mom tried to steal the basket from him. "Fina, you know me. I live in the moment."

This was an understatement. Mom was a spender and not a saver. My first two years of modeling money had gone to pay off her credit card debts. Subsequently, I never stopped contributing.

"Indeed," I replied.

"Maybe you wouldn't be so anxious if you didn't think about the future so much," Roxanne suggested.

"Really?"

"I was a philosophy major," she explained.

"Oh, wow. Did you study Wittgenstein, Hegel, and Kant?"

"Yep."

"You must be brilliant," I conceded.

Roxanne shrugged. "I'm a good test taker."

"Marie, I love Mexican food," Herman chimed in changing the subject.

"Well, I don't like Asian food," Mom explained.

"But, Marie, you've lived in Asia for decades," Roxanne said.

Mom nodded while downing her margarita too quickly. "Yes, but I only like fried rice and spring rolls."

I crossed my arms. "Mexican food is affordable in the U.S., but here it's a luxury item."

Herman mimicked me and mouthed *Debbie the downer*.

I kicked him hard under the table. "Shut up."

"Fina, what's wrong with you?" Mom demanded.

"Herman."

Roxanne looked at my enemy sympathetically. She then eyed me like a used car salesman. "Who was *that* guy you were with the other night?"

Her aggression intimidated me. "What guy?"

Herman snorted. "Don't play coy. The meathead with the tattoos."

I shrugged. "Just a guy."

"I didn't want to say anything," Mom interjected, "but I was *not* impressed."

Roxanne's eyes narrowed while she studied me like a beat cop interrogating a vagrant. "So, did you guys hook up?"

Roxanne puzzled me. She had everything I desired: an impressive education, an MBA from NYU, and an advertising executive position. Yet she was interested in very average men.

For example, the other night she'd asked about Herman. I was about to explain his crimes, but then stopped. I hoped she might take off with the guy. Then my family would finally be rid of him.

Herman's eyes lit up while Mom shook her head.

I wanted to scream, "None of your damned business!"

Instead, I kept calm. "Aaron joined Selina, Evelina, and I for drinks. I left early because I was tired."

"Oh, come on," Roxanne pressed. "We're adults. You can tell us what really happened."

I was sick of this woman's pushiness and wanted to smash Herman's taco across her face. "I just told you what happened."

I nibbled at my mango salsa salad. Someday, would I end up working for someone like Roxanne?

Mom interjected, "Aaron doesn't look like

your type."

"And your point would be?" I asked.

"Why waste your time with him?" Mom answered.

"It's a long story," I explained.

"We've got time," Herman piped in.

I exhaled. "A friend asked me to talk to him."

Mom chomped on her taco. Sauce dripped down her face. "Why?"

"Sorry, I can't divulge his secrets," I explained.

"Did Aaron call you?" Roxanne demanded.

"No," I replied. "I took off abruptly, which probably let him know I'm not interested."

Roxanne snorted. "I couldn't believe that guy's arms. He was so cut."

"I guess. My male model buddies are leaner."

"Fina, if he hasn't called by now, then he won't," Roxanne continued.

"Good to know," I replied.

The waitress began clearing plates. While the group ordered Mexican coffee and fried ice cream, I sat and watched with a sly grin. Who needed to murder this trio? They'd self-destruct on their own.

"If Aaron hasn't called, then that's for the best," Mom opined.

"Why?"

Herman cut in, "As I said before, he's a meathead."

"Aaron is intelligent. He's read all of Clavell's books, and he's an entrepreneur."

"What line of work?" Roxanne asked.

"Not sure," I lied. Changing the subject, I asked, "Didn't I go to I.S.B. with kids whose dads were in Vietnam?"

Mom shook her head. "I doubt it. Your classmates' fathers were paper pushers."

"What about Dan?"

"Who?"

"The guy who was stalking you? He dressed up as Santa for a holiday event. My best friend Kate and I were elves. So we had to work with him the entire day."

This was a perfect example of Mom attracting stalkers. She was too friendly.

Mom clasped a hand to her forehead. "Good God, Dan Turner."

"Wasn't he in Vietnam? He talked about it."

Mom shook her head. "Nah, I called the Embassy. Apparently, Dan performed menial clerical work. Putting paperclips on folders."

"Ah, so he was never in active combat?"

"Definitely not."

"Well, that's something for Aaron to be proud of. Any nerd can hide behind a desk. But it takes a real man to put himself on the front line."

Everyone groaned.

I suddenly felt sorrow for Aaron.

Thankfully, Herman changed the subject and

asked, "What about our upcoming trip to Laos?"

"Excuse me, I'm going to the washroom," I said. I needed to be alone.

The Sweet Salsa was within a luxury hotel, The Mandarin Silk. I decided to walk through and window shop. I paced up and down marble steps and across rooms with high-vault ceilings. Chandeliers made the place glow. I analyzed the worn oriental carpets while trying to think. The rugs had stories; I imagined the people who'd trampled across them.

I was frustrated by everyone's opinions. I don't think I'd eaten enough because my salad was too light. I'd swum too much earlier. Confusion gripped me because I suddenly had mixed feelings for Aaron.

A few hours ago, I was bored thinking about him and didn't care if I'd ever see him again. But Roxanne's pushiness, interest, and challenging nature sparked a competitive rage within me.
I checked my phone. In some ways, I liked the fact that Aaron didn't call, text, or email. I felt hounded when guys did that. The fact that he kept his distance made me almost like him. He was respectful and gave me plenty of space.

My mother's dismissal of Aaron created immeasurable pain. Why did she judge Aaron and not Herman or countless other contentious friends? Mom's dislike of the guy elevated my opinion of him. Mom favored people who shared her leftist views, which seemed limiting. I always thought my family was frustrating. Maybe Aaron's family was more complicated?

Aaron reminded me of Heathcliff, the Byronic hero from *Wuthering Heights*. Both had grown up struggling against adversity and applied ingenuity to transcend class barriers. Compared to my peers, Aaron seemed unique because he possessed an apparent strength.

They say a shared sense of humor is the key to a fruitful friendship. I was surrounded by people who either lacked one or didn't appreciate mine. I preferred to think the latter. Aaron was amused by anything I did or said, which made me incredibly happy.

And he read books for fun? Most of my childhood schoolmates only read assignments and played video games. Their arrogance reflected fear because they knew that they were marginal at best, or worse—products of the degenerate leisure classes dependent on their family's money. Indeed, after the banking crisis of 1997 and later 2008, many were reduced to poverty. Meanwhile, those they scorned acquired unimaginable wealth.

I was used to effeminate men, similar to Jane's childhood enemies in Charlotte Bronte's Jane Eyre, who couldn't handle women disagreeing with them. Confronting their delusional beliefs with sound logic was an attack on their ego, which typically produced ad hominem attacks. I saw this as the highest form of praise.

So far, Aaron didn't try to dominate me. He didn't have to. When I disagreed, argued, or challenged him, he just laughed. Most of my male peers would have flown into a rage and then emailed me a list of my deficiencies, which was generally more a reflection of them than me.

CHAPTER 17: HOURS LATER

I paced around my bedroom in my long white nightgown. I kept chanting, *You do not like Aaron. You must forget all about him. You do not have feelings for him. There is no emotional connection.*

I was trying to hypnotize myself, but it wasn't working. I couldn't sleep.

Not falling asleep was dangerous because Beelzebub could appear. As long as it was daytime or I was sleeping, I was safe.

The fact that Beelzebub hadn't appeared lately made me suspicious. Where was Bub? Why wasn't he here to scold me for fumbling my latest opportunity to murder Aaron?

So I hopped into bed, slid under the covers, and hugged my pillow. Thankfully, I quickly drifted to sleep.

Dream

I was back in eleventh-century Japan sitting on

the steps near my home watching a wren perched on a tree branch. I sighed. How I loved cherry blossom trees.

I was startled by a rustling in the bushes. It was the Samurai—again? This time I decided not to flee and remained calm.

There was a broken path among the fallen leaves. He took a few careful steps toward me and sat down. His armor seemed so overdone and out of place compared to my pale robes.

I remained still but peeked towards the gates. He offered me a single chrysanthemum.

Finally, I reacted. "You're not supposed to be here."

He grinned. "Why?"

"So many reasons."

"Like?"

"First of all, you're from a different century. This is the year 1001. You shouldn't appear for another six-hundred years.

"How well do you know your future?"

I was confused and said nothing.

"I think you mean two-hundred years."

I exhaled. "Samurai aren't supposed to be in my courtyard."

"Better to be a warrior in the garden than a gardener in a war."

"What? I think you missed my point."

"It's an old Samurai quote."

"And kind of common sense, don't you think?"

"Not for many."

I nodded. "Indeed."

He changed the subject. "Why are you so un-happy?"

"I'm not."

"I've been watching you for weeks."

I blinked. "How?"

"The emperor cares for you more than anyone."

"By that logic, you probably shouldn't be here."

"Then why aren't you happy?"

I tilted my head. "Why do you think the emperor loves me?"

"You're his favorite. Everyone knows it. He's obsessed with you."

"Obsession isn't love. It's control. I feel trapped."

"But you have so much power."

"To do what? Everyone hates me."

The Samurai smiled and inched closer. I immediately pulled back.

I sighed. "I think I'm dreaming."

He leaned forward. "You wouldn't be having this dream if you didn't care."

I swallowed and trembled at the sounds of heavy footsteps, a shrill fire alarm, and screaming. Was it the Imperial guards? We were both dead and would be burned alive.

I woke with anxiety. Where was I? What was happening? I opened my eyes and realized I was in bed. The sun shone brightly into my room. The fire alarm blared, and a burning scent permeated the house.

Khun Jai was screaming, "Madame, come quick."

Herman yelled, "Hey, my waffles are on fire!"

"Quick, grab the towel," Mom ordered.

Good God, I thought. *Do I live in a zoo or a circus? Considering the drama, I suspect the latter.*

I fell back into bed and contemplated my dream. Did it mean anything? Yes, I'd been reading *Lady Murasaki's Diary, The Tale of Genji,* and watching too many Zhang Yimou films. It certainly didn't mean that I had feelings for Aaron Walker, even though the Samurai in my dreams looked like him.

I willed myself to forget him.

But why had I been drawn to this artwork? Why did I feel a strong connection to the ancient Far East? Who was this Japanese woman I dreamt of? Was she a former life?

CHAPTER 18: THE FOLLOWING WEEK

I focused on packing for my return to Eugene. I'd leave in eight days. I felt numb, realizing I might never return to Bangkok. So I spent quality time with Selina and Evelina.

We were now at The Bamboo Hut, sitting by bamboo trees and a pond filled with water lilies. I watched a toad leap from a pad onto the bank. Pink flowers blew in the wind and landed in our teacups.

Evelina looked me in the eye. "Fina, what happened with you and that guy?"

I sipped my strawberry smoothie and played innocent. "What guy?"

Selina threw her head back. "C'mon, Fina. You know who we're talking about."

"You rarely like anyone," Evelina remarked.

"Sure, I do. I love our friends and Jess."

Selina shook her head. "Fina, you like Chad,

Jess, and the other male models as friends. It's not the same."

"I don't like Aaron."

Evelina continued, "Then why did you leave with him?"

I sighed. "It's a long story."

"We love stories," Selina exclaimed.

I nodded. "I know you do. I'll write soap operas."

"Yes, and I can be your actress," Selina said happily.

"Fina, you're a nerd," Evelina declared.

"Thank you."

"It's not a compliment."

"Okay."

"Forget writing about drama. Live it," Evelina finished.

"I can live vicariously through you," I suggested.

"Where did you go after you left?" Selina asked.

"The Pink Lotus," I replied.

Evelina rolled her eyes. "Boring."

"Yep, so I left."

"You left?" Selina asked. "Why?"

I shrugged. "Aaron is just like Jess. Just another player."

"Fina, you never give men a chance. You always storm off," Selina explained.

"If Aaron liked me, he would have called."

Evelina shook her head. "Not if you were an asshole like you typically are."

"Thank you," I replied. "Roxanne insists he didn't call because he's not into me."

Evelina groaned. "Why would you listen to *that* person?"

"Roxanne is brilliant. She majored in philosophy and even has an MBA."

Evelina rolled her eyes. "She's a nerd. She knows nothing about life."

I sighed. "Well, if anyone understands the human heart, it's the two of you."

I was surprised by my girlfriends' acceptance of Aaron. They typically idealized aristocrats and rarely appreciated my caution. I meant well and explained that old money marries old money. I wasn't sure if I should take dating advice from either. They favored local propaganda. I called this the Madame Bovary complex and determined that the distinction between film and books maintained the status quo. After all, in popular media, an average girl marries a tycoon. Whereas throughout classical literature, there was a timeless theme of men marrying women for money: Thomas Hardy's *Far From the Madding Crowd*, Henry James' *Wings of the Dove*, and Jean Rhys' *Wide Sargasso Sea*.

"You should call him," Evelina insisted.

"I can't."

Selina grabbed my phone. "Yes, you can."

"Stop." I wailed.

Evelina snatched my phone, scrolled through the numbers, and dialed Aaron's.

I yelped and fought for my phone. But it was too late because Evelina had already called Aaron. Luckily, I ended it before he answered.

Within seconds, I received a text from Aaron: *Hey, did you call? I'm driving through some pretty bad traffic.*

"What did he say?" the girls asked.

I flashed them the text. But then I wrote back: *That was an accident! I never call people.*

Aaron immediately wrote back: *Ha, ha.*

I showed the texts to my girlfriends. They shook their heads. "Fina, you can't end it like that."

I shrugged. "What should I say?"

Selina suggested, "Tell him you're leaving soon."

Evelina agreed, "Yeah, tell him you want to meet and say goodbye."

I managed a weak smile. "I'll think about it."

"What do you have to think about?" Evelina demanded.

"I'm not sure if I *should* see Aaron again."

"Why?" Selina asked.

I sighed. "What would be the point?"

Evelina lectured, "You never take risks. You hide behind a book instead of being in front of the camera, like us. So, what if you only see Aaron one more time? That's life. Nothing lasts forever, but you should try to have some fun before you leave."

"Maybe you're right."

"Someday, you're going to be an old lady with one-hundred cats," Evelina continued.

"You say that like it's a bad thing," I joked.

Luckily, before Evelina could say anything else, we were interrupted by a slender woman with jet-black hair and a creamy tofu complexion.

"Fina?" she exclaimed, giving me a big hug.

"Do I know you?" I asked with surprise.

"I was your stand-in at Nivea TVC."

Evelina and Selina waved hello. The three seemed to know each other.

My eyes widened. "I can't believe you were my stand-in. You're so pretty."

She smiled. "You were always so quiet."

"I was?"

"Yes, you never said a word. You always had your head in a book."

Evelina and Selina laughed.

"But you were always such a lady," she finished.

"Thank you, but I wish I were more like you," I responded. For a second, I felt overwhelmed with guilt. What had become of me? A few weeks ago, I smeared cake all over Herman. The other evening, I kicked him in the shin. I was moody, frustrated, and now chasing Aaron? What next? Could I sink any lower? Yes, hopefully. Ladies are elegant, but it was too much work. After all, the role of a genuine lady is to be gentle, kind, and make people feel at ease. Elegant ladies went to Heaven! I'd already been there, and it wasn't fun. Forget that, I wanted adventure.

CHAPTER 19: THURSDAY

August in Bangkok was generally wet. Monsoons frequently ravaged the city during this season while snails congregated on sidewalks. However, this year it was unusually dry. The rains rarely fell, which created discord amongst everyone since so much of life depends upon water.

I had given up on hearing from Aaron. It was for the best because I needed to move on with my life. My future would never be in South East Asia, so it was better not to get too attached. Selina and I spent our Thursday afternoon swimming and working out at Clark Hatch. Afterward, we ventured downtown to complete some shopping. I was in a taxi returning home from the mall when I received a text. I glanced down and was surprised to discover the message was from Aaron:

Hey Fina, Friday is my last night in town. Having a party at the casino. Come.

I didn't respond and didn't think I should. A party at The Hibiscus? That sounded seedy. It's where I had met him, and it hadn't felt so bad at the time. But I think the greater issue was that this last-minute invite felt highly disingenuous.

As I walked into the house, I observed Roxanne and Herman. They were sharing popcorn while watching *Alien*. I was still annoyed by Roxanne's harsh interrogation. The emotionally- undeveloped primitive side of me needed to show her up. I needed to let her know that despite her doubts, Aaron was still interested in me. After all, this was a competition, right?

I hit the pause button. "Sorry to interrupt," I lied. I wasn't sorry at all. I hoped that I was now interfering in these love birds' frolic. The sight of two people engaged in a romantic rendezvous, even one as casual as viewing a popular film unnerved me. How dare anyone have fun or enjoy life? At least, not when I was stressed and unhappy. I suddenly realized that I was still a demon. A wry grin emerged across my face.

"What's up?" they asked, looking up.

I paused for a few moments in an attempt to build suspense.

"What is it?" Roxanne snapped. Her abrasive body language had frightened me a few weeks ago. Now, her brazen tone pleased me.

"Yeah, we're trying to watch a movie," Herman added.

I swallowed and looked from side to add a dramatic effect.

"I'm turning *Alien* back on," Roxanne threatened.

"Aaron texted," I bragged with a smug air.

I shouldn't have been so open, but I couldn't resist gloating to Roxanne. Her forehead furrowed while Herman raised an eyebrow.

"So, what? Who cares?" asked Herman.

"Took him long enough," Roxanne retorted.

Foolishly, I couldn't stop showing off. "Yeah, so Aaron wants to meet at The Hibiscus. There's a party Friday night."

Neither seemed to care and ignored me. Herman turned *Alien* back on.

Mom was walking down the stairs and overheard our conversation. She hit pause

"Look, girls, I don't want to be the bearer of bad news, but you know how men are when they come to Asia."

"Like Dad?" Roxanne asked.

"Sure," Mom agreed. "The local girls make them feel like gods. So, Fina, forget this Aaron guy."

"The local girls only care about money," Roxanne suggested. I figured she was harboring bitterness over her parents' divorce. I had grown up seeing so many ex-pat marriages ravished by an interloper. I should have felt empathy for Roxanne, but I didn't.

"Yes, these women are predators," Mom agreed.

"Exactly, it's the bulge in the back of a guys'

pants these birds want, not the front," Herman asserted with a sneer. I had an overwhelming desire to punch him but suppressed the urge.

I heard the voice of a former fellow angel whisper, "Fina, darling, resorting to violence is neither elegant nor ladylike." I crossed my arms to conceal the tension growing throughout my body. "Of course, these women only want money. What else is there to desire?"

No one said anything for a few minutes. The three just stared at me.

Finally, Mom broke the silence. "The local girls don't love foreigners. They bewitch men, break up families, steal money, and then keep a local guy on the side."

"Yeah," Roxanne agreed. "They're gold-diggers. Wanton little man thieves."

"So, what," I stated firmly.

"So, what? What kind of morals do you possess?" Mom demanded.

"None," I declared flippantly. *Once a demon, always a demon, I thought. It doesn't matter if I'm a part of Hell or not.*

Roxanne's eyes narrowed while Herman's widened. He seemed intrigued.

I continued, "Maybe love is the problem."

"Huh?" Roxanne asked.

Suddenly the voices of my former lives were breaking through. I felt more like my genuine self and less like the drone created by this neo-colonial hypocritical ex-pat community. "It's always been a man's world. For thousands of years, women sought comfort from one another and not men. I'm not condoning the actions of women who break up families. But they're in survival mode."

"Fina, what is your point?" Mom demanded.

"Of course these women want money, but what do you expect?"

Mom sighed. "For them to respect the sanctity of marriage."

I shrugged. "Sure, but if all they want is money, then why are they such a threat? Their needs are very basic."

Herman's eyes narrowed.

"You don't make any sense!" Roxanne declared.

I exhaled and sat down. "Relationships are rarely permanent."

"That's so cynical," Roxanne retorted. "I go in thinking that a relationship will last forever."

And something tells me they never do, I thought sardonically.

Mom shook her head. "Fina, I'm not sure what you're going on about. But I think you're wasting your time with Aaron."

"The guy looks like pure sleaze," Herman interjected.

Mom continued, "Because he's probably got a local girlfriend he adores. She's probably sweet and devoted to him in a way you could never be."

What was Mom doing? Waving a red flag in front of my nose as if we were in Madrid?

I was born a contrarian. When I was three, the electricity went out. Mom went off with Dad to check the fuse box. I was left alone by a large candle. My parents repeatedly told me not to touch the candle. So what did I do after they'd left for five-minutes? I tipped it over. Soon my entire body was covered in hot wax. I screamed, and they ran back.

One minute Mom was cutting Aaron down. The next, she was suggesting I couldn't get him because of local competition. Ha! Now I was almost determined. I was George W. Bush, and Aaron Walker was Saddam Hussein. But I wasn't about to fall for the bait. Aaron wasn't worth it. I had no desire to text him back or attend his lame party. What would be the point? So I could ask him more questions while he barely had anything to say?

But I wasn't about to leave the living room without further annoying everyone. Dramatically in jest, I performed a scene from *Wuthering Heights*. It was a scene I'd rehearsed repeatedly as a teenager. I clasped my hand to my chest, threw my head back, and exclaimed, "I am Heathcliff. He's more myself than I am. Whatever our souls are made of, his and mine are the same."

No one was impressed, so Roxanne hit the play button. *Alien* resumed.

As I skipped upstairs, I heard Mom opine, "Fina

should stop watching those old classic films.
She's too much of a romantic. It's not realistic at all."

I heard Herman snort. "Yeah, she doesn't understand men."

While venturing into my bedroom, I pondered my recent attempt at satire. As always, no one seemed to get my humor. What did Emily Bronte mean when she wrote: *I am Heathcliff?* Did she genuinely feel that he was her soul mate? Or did she mean that Heathcliff was her? Isn't it funny that women created the male characters who enchant women for centuries?

Aaron's party was tomorrow, Friday night. But I had no plans to attend. I let Mom, Roxanne, and Herman think I'd go, simply to rile them up. So I fixated on getting ready for bed. I figured I'd wake early to get in a serious workout and finish packing.

As I crawled into bed, I closed my eyes, hoping to hear the words of a former life. But there was only silence. I breathed deeply and tried again. Nothing. So I picked up Lady Murasaki's diary and began reading. Soon I fell asleep.

I was back in eleventh-century Japan. It was the Heian period, when women educated in seventh-century Chinese literature were allowed a share of the inheritance and even had their own homes. It was a high period of literature written mostly by women, includ-

ing Lady Murasaki.

I now remembered who I had been. I was an adviser to the ruling family—the Fujiwara clan. I was at court where a brilliant assemblage of nobles was congregated at a ceremony. At the center, musicians played string instruments. It was a festival, and I wore pale pastel-colored robes: sherbet, lavender, and periwinkle.

I walked through the court with too much confidence. There was an excessive bounce in my step. I felt the severe gazes of high officials observing my giddiness, which might befit a schoolgirl, but certainly not a noblewoman.

I felt a cold hand clasp my wrist, so I stopped and gasped. It was Lady Saisho. She leaned in and whispered into my ear, "Dear, your robes and scarves are not so bad, but they're a little too bright."

Instantly my cheeks colored as I felt slighted. The Heian period was characterized by exquisite taste with a substantial emphasis on fashion and poetry. Wearing the wrong shade of color was the height of poor breeding and bad manners.

I said to Lady Saisho, "Goodness gracious, whatever shall I do?"

While she answered with a slight gleam of satisfaction, I noticed the samurai who looked precisely like Aaron in the distance. He was lingering in the corner with his extremely muscular arms crossed. Amusement crossed his face, and he chuckled. It's as if he was thinking, Who cares?

While Lady Saisho continued her gentle reprim-

and, I silently thought, Because I've lost my objective. I no longer know why I'm here. This Heian period is so boring.

Later that evening, after the ceremony, I was alone in the garden outside of my home. I sat on the steps listening to the rippling of water while watching the chrysanthemum leaves fall.
A crescent moon glowed in the black sky while an owl surveyed the terrain.

Aaron sat down beside me and whispered, "Give me the Governor's maps, and I'll take you away."

I had no intention of doing so but played along. "Which maps?"

"The ones detailing the distant provinces and minor posts."

"Is that all?"

"And the Governor's schemes for office."

"What makes you think he has any?"

Aaron narrowed his eyes. "C'mon, no one leaves Kyoto happily. Everyone schemes for higher office."

I nodded but stood up and backed away.

"Hey, where are you going?" *he demanded.*

I started to run through the courtyard and toward the Governor's building. I had to warn the Fujiwara family. Aaron jumped to his feet and chased after me. I ran faster but tripped over my robes. As I fell to the ground, I felt him overpower me. He gripped his large hand around my tiny neck and strangled me to death before I could warn anyone. Then Aaron confiscated secret documents hidden in the deep pockets of my robes.

It was the end of that former life.

I jolted awake, feeling feverish. It was still dark as I tried to ascertain the meaning of my dream. In a former life, Aaron had been a spy from one of two military families, the Taira and Minamoto. They eventually rose to power and replaced a peaceful civilization with a highly militaristic one.

It was now clear what I had to do. I had to avenge my murderer. I had to kill Aaron. So I reached for the phone sitting on my night table and texted: *See you tonight.*

Aaron immediately replied: *Can't wait.*

I'll bet, I thought smugly.

CHAPTER 20:
FRIDAY NIGHT

The sky was black but lit by a full moon. The scent of danger lingered.

I'd eaten as much fruit as humanly possible so that I would have energy for the party. The excessive amount of banana and pineapple sugar kept me satiated while I spent hours getting ready.

After a lavender-scented bubble bath, I set my hair in rollers. I methodically applied makeup with an emphasis on my cat-like eyes and cupid's bow mouth. I then slipped into my new dress. It was gold with a heart-shaped bodice. The waist was tapered tight and billowed into ruffles, which revealed my twenty-four-inch waist. This ballerina-style dress was ideal for an hour-glass figure.

Was my routine excessive? Absolutely, but this was war. I couldn't walk into Aaron's casino party looking like a killer. It best I appear as unsuspecting as possible. I slipped a very delicate but extremely sharp blade into my purse, which I'd slice into Aaron's neck later that evening when he had his guard down.

I then took out my rollers and styled my hair into an updo. I doused myself in a floral fragrance and slipped into my clear slipper high heels and pranced down the stairs like a schoolgirl on her way to Prom. As I dashed into the living room, I was startled and stopped. Mom had passed out on the couch.

I tiptoed over. She looked almost dead. I then observed a big empty tray of brownies. I gripped her wrist and felt for a pulse. I was relieved to discover that she was alive. I shrugged, figuring she'd overeaten and would eventually wake up around midnight. It was now only 9:00 p.m.

I was anxious to attend the party. Thus, I raced out the door into the warm evening air, which smelled crisp. The scent of mango from the tropical trees around back lingered while the sounds of cars whizzing by overpowered the soft rippling water in the creek. A small lizard hopped past my feet.

I was about to open the heavy iron gate when I heard a deep voice croak, "Stop. Don't make a move."

I froze. "Herman," I whispered. "Is that you?" As I carefully spun around, I gasped.

In the shadows near the pillars on our porch, Herman was holding Dr. Blackie by the scruff of the neck. In his other hand he held a carving knife.

I started to wobble in my heels. I was frantic and stammered, "Please! Please, don't hurt Dr. Blackie."

"Not another word or the cat loses his head."

I gasped and bit my lip but remained silent.

"Fina, get inside the house, now!"

Oh, my God, I thought while following my enemy back into our house. Herman was still gripping Blackie tightly.

I looked into Blackie's golden eyes and said with my own eyes, *Hang in there, little buddy.*

"Fina, sit down." Herman pulled out a chair. Reluctantly, I followed his orders.

Herman locked the door. He then put a laundry basket over Blackie and secured it with an iron. My childhood ally was trapped. This was my moment to escape, but I dared not risk it.

Herman must have read my mind. He picked up a chair and threatened, "Try anything, and I'll stomp Blackie with this!"

Unfortunately, my captor ripped my purse from out of my hands. I had hoped to pry it open to retrieve my blade. Herman then tied my legs together, placed my hands around the back of the chair, and secured my wrists.

I thought, *Wow, Herman's been planning this for the last twenty-four hours. The fact that he stole a laundry basket from out back—where Khun Jai washes clothes—and hid it behind Mom's oriental screen proves his modus operandi. What a little worm! He's even more calculating than I imagined. Maybe he planned this crime all summer?*

"Please, please," I begged. "Please don't hurt Dr. Blackie."

"He's fine, Fina."

"We're both tied up."

"Exactly."

"Why are you doing this?"

"Many reasons."

"Like…"

Herman paced around the room. His carrot-colored locks were messy and overgrown. He wore an oversized yellow shirt and jeans. "First, I'm sick of you and your bullshit, Fina. You must be punished."

"Okay."

"Second, I don't think you should see Aaron again."

"Why?"

"What are you planning to do?" Herman demanded with a sneer.

"Talk," I replied.

"Yeah, right. Do you think a guy like that asks you to meet him in the seediest part of town to talk?"

I shrugged and joked, "Most men want my mind, not my body."

He rolled his eyes and shook his head. "You're so naïve, Fina."

"You know everything, right?" I replied, but I silently thought, *The most dangerous predators are the ones you least suspect.*

In my previous lives, including this one, I trained in the art of diplomacy. In each life, I grew up studying ballet, oil painting, and literature while my peers trained for battle. I didn't have to use my body because I was like Scheherazade of 1001 Arabian Nights, who conquered a misogynistic King by telling him a different story each night.

It was never difficult to keep powerful men at bay. Why? Because men who can obtain women too easily seek something else. It takes time to build relationships, but when one does, she can advise generals like Hannibal to cross the alps using elephants. Or to encourage Napoleon, George Washington, and Ho Chi Minh to resort to guerilla warfare.

Herman was still shuffling about. He seemed more confident than usual, but only marginally so. It was apparent that this hostage business was stressful on him. "Why do you like Aaron so much?"

I swallowed. "You'll never understand."

"Try me."

My body tensed. "This is none of your business!"

"It is now," Herman croaked with a chuckle.

"What happened to Mom?" I asked, changing the subject while turning my head and glancing at the couch.

"She ODed on marijuana brownies."

"Are you serious?"

"Yep. I gave her the tray, and she scarfed it down in minutes."

I exhaled. "Sounds like Mom." She had never failed to resist a baked good.

Herman continued, "She'll be out for hours."

"Herman, I just wanted to say goodbye to Aaron."

Yeah, right.

This is none of your business, I thought angrily. Diplomatically, I lied, "I need to tell Aaron I'm sorry." I was frustrated by my predicament but determined to break free. While I engaged Herman in petty banter, I worked hard to untie the ropes around my wrists, which were behind me and out of sight from my captor.

"For what?"

"It's hard to explain."

"That's another thing, Fina. We're all sick of your explaining."

I nodded.

Herman narrowed his eyes. "Everything is always about you."

"Sure."

"If you were a truly confident woman, you wouldn't wear makeup."

"Absolutely."

"Look at you! All dolled up. For what, a guy?"

I exhaled but didn't respond.

Herman continued, "You're no feminist."

"I guess not."

"You need to love yourself."

I cringed and wanted to vomit. "Wow, that's an original platitude."

"Hey!" Herman shouted. He wielded a knife at me, narrowly missing my nose.

"Sorry, you're so wise." But silently I thought, *You groupie. You sound like a bumper sticker and belong in a self-help cult.*

"You're real snarky, aren't you, Fina?"

"I'm just trying to be funny."

"Yeah, well, you're not."

"Comedy is difficult," I conceded.

"It's because you don't love yourself."

"Yeah, for sure." *Oh, brother,* I thought. *When will this guy quit with the love stuff?*

"You're rude and sarcastic."

I bit my lip to keep from saying, *It's every woman's dream to meet a guy who talks like a meme. Aloud, I agreed* "Sure."

"If you truly loved yourself, then you wouldn't dress like this, wear makeup or deodorant."

"Uh-huh."

"You wouldn't shave your legs either."

I nodded. "Yes, it takes a powerful woman to do that. I hide behind camouflage."

Herman swallowed. "Now, we're getting somewhere. For once, you're honest."

I exhaled. "There are so many self-assured

women out there who don't need makeup. Why not focus on them?"

"Because you need my help. Fina, I'm trying to help you be the best version of yourself.

"Sure," I lied. I thought, *I'm firmly committed to being the worst person possible. Who died and made you God?*

Instantly, I had a revelation. God seemed authoritative. Yet had he ever told me what to do? If I felt guilty, that was on me. Even Raphael never used the trite platitudes Herman regurgitated. Did I miss Heaven? If I felt pressure amongst the angels, maybe it was self-induced. At least God made it clear he didn't want anyone preaching. He warned of false prophets and people who publicly branded their religion.

What right did anyone, least of all a stoner like Herman, have to tell others who they should be? I wanted to smack him or kick him in the face. This was good. The rush of adrenalin kept me from falling asleep.

Herman shuffled around the room. "You're so self-absorbed. Now, for once, it's all about me."

"Okay."

"You know my dad is Russian, right?"

"Yes," I lied. I possessed a photographic memory, but conveniently forgot any details concerning Herman's life.

"The guy was a jerk."

"Uh-huh."

"Mom wasn't great either. One time she forgot to pick me up from school. What kind of mother does that?"

My mind wandered while Herman yapped away. I thought about an incident almost ten years ago that wasn't too dissimilar from the one now.

Flashback

It was a hot summer, and I was twelve. I lay in bed fighting a fever. Mom was at work while Dad was away on business. Khun Jai wasn't around.

Mom's pushy friend Lydia barged into my bedroom with her daughter, Tania.

Lydia offered me a glass of water. "You're sick?"

I woke. "What are you doing here?"

"I got into a fight with my husband."

"I'm sorry to hear that."

We were abruptly interrupted by screaming. I jolted alert. "It's Kitty." Immediately, I jumped up and raced outside.

My younger sister was running while crying. Tears streamed down her face. She was traumatized while carrying a dead puppy covered in blood.

Behind Kitty was our security guard. He held a bloody club and was about to beat another one of her dogs to death.

Lydia and Tania became hysterical. Our Polish and Japanese neighbors emerged from their homes; both women were stoic like me.

I kept my cool but shook my head with disbelief.

"That man works for us."

Maybe I didn't react because I'd grown up visiting my father's factories focused on meat production. Dad's workers were as meek as the carcasses hanging from hooks. Or maybe my response was characteristic of an adolescent demon.

No one said anything. I was frustrated, wondering why this was allowed to happen. I couldn't believe this guard's disrespect for my family. Certainly this wouldn't have happened if my father was home.

"How can he do this? He works for us."

Tania screamed, "Fina, you've already said that."

I was annoyed. How dare my mother's friends barge into my home and attack me? I was trying to be hospitable, but now I had to deal with the staff's insubordination and confront brazen reprimands? Where were my parents? Why did they allow such nonsense?

Things rarely bothered me after that incident. In junior high, the boys joked that I was a psychopath because nothing they said mattered. Indeed, I was emotionally unavailable and cold-tempered. Open discussions regarding people's feelings seemed peculiar.

High school and the modeling world—sources of discontent for many—were a reprieve for me. If my peers or competition created conflict, I barely noticed. I had other battles to fight.

***

I raised my head slightly and peeked at the

clock above the door. It was chiming as it did every hour. This clock was like Dr. Blackie—something I'd grown so accustomed to that I took it for granted. I didn't appreciate either as much as I should have. My cat's whimpering distressed me. It was one thing for Herman to hate me, but hurting an innocent creature was unforgivable. I tried to catch Blackie's eye, but his gaze was troubled and unfocused. He was old. No doubt, this ordeal was causing unspeakable suffering. What if he died tonight due to the trauma of Herman's madness? Herman was a dead man. I continued struggling with the ropes, but the ones around my wrists wouldn't loosen. Luckily, the ones around my ankles didn't feel too tight. I had powerful legs thanks to ballet, running, and swimming.

The clock was the only thing to interrupt Herman's ranting and raving. Each hour, it chimed to indicate the time. Every half hour, it would ding once. It was strange Mom never woke, but she was out cold.

Herman had been blabbering for almost two hours, and it was torture. Perspiration dripped from my once perfect updo. My dress felt sweaty, and my throat was parched. I started to yawn and nod off. I was so sick of listening to Herman and his whiney stories about his tough childhood. The worst part was when he started reciting cryptic poetry. It was flowery and rarely made any sense. Sometimes it included direct, personal attacks at me.

I wanted to scream, "Grow up. You didn't have a dad or a perfect life. So what? Neither did anyone else. No one cares. You grew up in a nation people risk their lives to live in." Ninety percent of the inhabitants in this world would kill for the opportunities Herman had inherited. He lived in one of the world's best cities, had fresh water, clean air, and free education. And what did Herman do with his life? He became a full-fledged criminal. A sharp pain stabbed through my head. Herman was still shuffling around performing his monologue. My wrists and legs ached from lack of movement. The tight ropes created swelling. A fly buzzed around my nose, but I sighed with relief because mosquitoes did not devour my bare flesh as they ordinarily would on any other occasion. Maybe it was the dry weather or my home's insulation coupled with our cold air-conditioning.

I was so frustrated. Why wouldn't Mom wake up?

Herman paused briefly to analyze me. "Fina, are you listening to me?"

I nodded. "Absolutely."

"What did I say?"

"Your mom's idea of gourmet cooking was burnt toast?"

Herman's face tensed and he practically jumped up and down. "No, that's not what I said. You haven't heard a word I've said, have you?"

I swallowed. "I'm sorry. It's just that I'm so tired."

For a split second, Herman actually looked sympathetic. "Fina, someday you'll thank me for this."

"I will?" I asked weakly.

"Yes, I'm protecting you."

"How?" I looked at my incarcerated cat. A moth flew outside his laundry basket cage. Ordinarily, Blackie would have been enchanted by a flying insect. Instead, he stared listlessly into space.

Herman's eyes widened like a mad man. "Fina, I'm saving you from yourself and a predatorial guy like Aaron. I'm your knight in shining armor."

"Thank you," I lied. "You're a regular Sir Lancelot."

"Huh? Who?"

"Never mind."

Herman's mouth tightened, and he shook his knife at me. "Are you being glib, again?"

"Goodness, no. I would never."

"Yeah, right."

I sighed. "Would you like to hear a story?"

Herman paused and sat down. He looked exhausted from talking all night. "Sure."

"Remember the statute that you broke?"

"The one you broke, Fina?"

"Yes, of course. During the Tang Dynasty, Yang Gui Fei was the Emperor's most beloved concubine. She was curvy, which was the ideal body type during that era."

Herman shrugged. "So?"

"She was blamed for exerting too much influence over the kingdom. Thus, the Emperor was forced to sacrifice her during a rebellion."

"That's not cool."

"Indeed," I agreed. "The story of Yang Guifei, had been romanticized in Asian history for hundreds of years. I'm not sure why. If the Emperor had genuinely cared for Guifei he would have fought to protect her and not had her strangled to death."

"Exactly," Herman replied.

I shook my head and bit my lip. My delusions regarding Aaron were ludicrous, yet they felt so real. Did I need to murder him? After all, I was not an assassin and had technically never killed anyone before. All I needed to know was the truth. I wanted to see Aaron again so I could confront him and learn more about what he knew, even if it meant threatening him with serious bodily injury. I yawned again. My heart raced, and my head throbbed from dehydration. The room seemed blurry. I was losing my grip on reality. At the same time, everything was becoming apparent. I was remembering my past lives and history as Lucifina. During the Middle Ages, I had softened my brother. He stopped wanting to destroy Earth and focused on making Hell a better place. Life in the nether world became more pleasant. Satan even turned down the fires. Everyone seemed happier. Everyone, except for one particular demon. Beelzebub flew into a rage.

I batted my eyes. They felt slightly sticky. What was going to happen to us? Where was the security guard? Should I scream and hope the neighbors heard me? Was Herman going to let us go? He was certifiably insane, right? Why didn't Mom listen to me? Why did she let this creep stay with us? I was being ridiculous. For years, I played the damsel in distress in television commercials and music videos where a muscular male hero rescued me. But that was never reality. Throughout my life, whenever I had been under attack, the ones to help me were either women, the natives, or myself.

My captor stopped. "Fina, Earth to Fina."

I fought to sit upright. "Sorry, what?"

"You spaced out there."

I nodded. "Yes, I'm terribly tired and thirsty."

"You were telling me a story."

Suddenly, I exclaimed, "Herman, I can't believe I allowed a Minamoto spy to strangle me to death in a former life."

His eyes widened. "What the heck are you talking about?"

I stammered, "One-thousand years ago, Japan was a thriving civilization built on peace. I swore to advise and protect the Fujiwara family by keeping the military families at bay. But I grew bored and craved excitement. In exchange, for the promise of adventure, I reconnoitered with an enemy intent on stealing the Fujiwara family's maps and governing secrets."

Herman raised an eyebrow as if questioning my sanity. "Huh? Another story?"

"I was a trusted adviser and had access to the Governor's office. I betrayed everyone by keeping the documents in my robes, which the Minamoto spy found and stole. I should have buried them under the Chrysanthemum tree."

"Yeah, that's not cool."

I nodded. "If I hadn't been so careless with the confidential documents, they wouldn't have been stolen. Maybe Japan would never have become so highly militaristic and invaded Korea, Manchuria, and South East Asia. It's all my fault. Once feudalism began, Satan and the rest of Hell changed. Everything returned to what it had been."

Herman's forehead furrowed and his green eyes widened. "Fina, are you okay?"

I blinked innocently. "Yes, why do you ask?"

"This is the wackiest story I've ever heard."

"The truth generally is."

Herman shook his head and stood up. "Do you seriously expect me to believe this?"

"Yes."

"Fina, I think you're delirious or something."

I nodded meekly. "Yes, I am. I'm so thirsty.

Can you please fetch me a glass of water from the kitchen."

"Sure," Herman agreed. As soon as he turned his back to me, I slipped my legs out from the ropes tied around my legs and sprung to my feet. I had been loosening them all night. My hands remained tied behind my back, but it made little difference.

I then gave Herman a big kick in the back of the head.

"Hey!" he wailed, but before he could turn around. I kicked him again. This time he started to fall over.

"You weren't a boy scout, were you?"

Herman was now on the floor and quite groggy. "No."

"Ha, no wonder. You're bad at tying knots. I should know, I was a girl scout."

"You don't act like one."

"Indeed, because most girl scouts wouldn't do what I'm about to do now." I was about to ram my stiletto heel into Herman's right eye when I heard my mother screaming.

Mom was now fully awake. "Fina, what are you doing?"

"Oh, hello, Mother. How nice of you to join us," I quipped while standing on top of Herman so he couldn't move.

"Fina, stop," Herman pleaded.

"I've got you right where you belong."

Mom rushed over. "For heaven's sake, what's

going on here?"

"What does it look like? Untie me."

Mom grabbed a pair of antique scissors from across the room sitting on her chestnut desk and then cut the ropes.

Once she finished, I exclaimed, "Quick, Mom, hand me the scissors."

"Why?" she asked, clutching them firmly to her body.

"So I can stab Herman in the eye."

"No," Herman wailed.

"No, Fina, we can't," Mom insisted.

"Fine, then we need to tie him up and call the police."

After we finished securing Herman, I anxiously removed the laundry basket from Dr. Blackie and attempted to cuddle him, but given the circumstances, he reacted more like a feral cat and less like a domesticated cat.

Dr. Blackie ravenously gulped water from his bowl. His breathing had increased, and his fur was disheveled.

After downing a glass of water, I raced upstairs to freshen up. The events of the evening had only fueled my intensity. The surge of adrenaline was like ten cups of coffee. Wound up, I needed to get out, and I needed to confront Aaron.

I headed for the door.

"Fina, where are you going?" Mom demanded.

"The party."

"At this hour?"

"Yes, it's important."

"Let me drive you."

I shook my head. "Thanks, but it's best if you keep an eye on ginger-locks and wait for the police."

Mom looked annoyed. "Okay, but I'd rather you be here when the police arrive."

I sauntered out the door. "Sure, we'd all like a lot of things in life, wouldn't we, mother? But I've done enough this evening. You'll have to take over now."

CHAPTER 21:
THE MIDDLE OF
THE NIGHT

I dashed outside into the tropical summer air. A warm breeze blew through my hair. I noted a full moon high in the sky. There was mostly silence except for the faint howling of my neighbor's dalmatians. Was I being selfish leaving mother alone with Herman and forcing her to contend with the police? Absolutely. But where had being a nice, dutiful daughter ever gotten me? Tied up by a maniac and lectured to for hours? Now I was late for my battle. I scurried to the edge of my compound while ambulances and police cars blazed past me. Within ten minutes, I got lucky and caught a taxi. We practically sailed through the streets since there was no traffic. During the drive, I observed the city, lit up like glitter. My heart raced, and I struggled to breathe properly. It was so late. Would Aaron still be at the party?

I unfastened my purse and pulled out my cell phone so I could explain I'd arrive soon. But it was impossible to text because my phone wouldn't power on. The battery had died during my imprisonment. I exhaled and attempted to calm down. *Don't worry, Fina. Aaron is a night owl. He'll still be there. Then you can finally tie up any loose ends.* In the past few days, I'd lost focus and was overwhelmed with packing. It was unlikely I'd return to a place I'd long called home. Our townhouse reminded me of a scene from *Pride and Prejudice* as Mom wrapped her antiques in boxes.

During the excitement, I'd allowed Roxanne and my mother's comments to fuel my competitive desire to prove them wrong. Why did I care what Mom or Roxanne thought? Was this all a distraction from my real problems—the trials and tribulations of being a young adult?

Thankfully, last night's dream and tonight's ordeal had woken me. I was still a demon even without Hell's backing because I was a rebel. When Satan and his cohorts had fought the war in Heaven, it was for freedom. But soon, my brother and the other demons became even more oppressive. I was fiercely independent and true to my ideals, as questionable as they might be. I didn't allow anyone to tell me who I should be or what to believe. I questioned everything and consistently desired to be in control of my own life. No one liked this, not anyone in Heaven, Hell, or even on

Earth, but that was not my problem. I didn't get up every day to answer or please anyone.

The taxi pulled up to The Hibiscus. I handed the driver too much money, insisting he keep the change. I hopped out and pranced up the steps like a ravenous squirrel on a nut hunt.

I breathed rapidly while dashing into the casino hall. The venue was barren because the party was past its apex.

The manager approached. "Can I help you?"

"Aaron Walker invited me to his party."

"Please wait, have a seat. I'll check."

I didn't sit, as the manager suggested. I watched him climb upstairs to the ballroom where *50 Cent* blasted. Party patrons were staggering out. Drunk couples hugged the perimeter because they could barely stand upright.

The atmosphere felt seedy. It smelled of cigarettes, alcohol, and regret.

I paced back and forth, hoping my target would appear.

He didn't, and neither did the manager.

I checked my reflection in the mirror. Despite tonight's ordeal, my makeup and hair were still intact. My face even glowed from the excitement.

I gazed upstairs and all around. I wanted to check the time, but I wore no watch. My phone had died, and there were no clocks in the casino.

My heart was pounding while my hands

trembled. I breathed rapidly and clasped my neck, where a bead of sweat formed.

Carefully, I crept up the stairs, waltzed toward the ballroom, and peeked inside. My pulse quickened.

The manager saw me and rushed up. "I'm sorry, miss, but Aaron Walker left."

The words sliced me like a blade because now I wouldn't be able to avenge my enemy.

After a few seconds, I stammered, "Did he leave a note or say anything?"

"No, miss."

"Will he return?"

"Probably not. Aaron went back to Macao."

"Thank you," I responded, looking down.

I exhaled and slowly glided down the stairs. The Hibiscus felt even more toxic as I absorbed wrath, sorrow, and sweat. There was a burst of energy in my chest. I wasn't about to give up this easily.

I marched out of the entrance, strolled down the steps, and lingered toward the back of the casino. I paused to gaze at the terrace overlooking the river. The water resembled oil under the moonlight. It was deceptively calm except for an occasional riverboat trudging through the inky liquid.

My eyes narrowed. This was where Aaron and I had played chess.

I peered at the wooden boardwalk lit up by a single light.

A sharp wind blew through my hair and cut my chest like a razor. I shivered. If only I'd kept my mouth shut yesterday. If only I'd kept my plans a secret. Why did I have to say anything to Herman?

I heard a noise. Startled, I stopped talking to myself and spun around. There was movement lurking in the shadows, but then a dark, muscular figure emerged. Was it Aaron? My heart raced. Maybe he hadn't left after all. Cautiously, I crept toward the corner.

CHAPTER 22: BEFORE DAWN

I gasped. "Beelzebub, I wasn't expecting to see you."

He grinned while approaching. His red eyes bulged against his tan skin. A vein in his neck protruded while he clenched his jaw.

I took a step backward and wrapped my arms around my body.

"Lucifina, once again, you botched an operation."

Beelzebub's words didn't sting nearly as much as the ones I'd said to myself. He didn't need to tell me I'd screwed up. I already knew it.

I exhaled and played along. "Please, you have to understand. I was completely ill-prepared for this investigation. If I'd had more time to research, then—"

Beelzebub stopped. "This wasn't an investigation. All you had to do was kill Aaron. A straightforward task."

My lips quivered. "I agree."

"It was so easy. You could have done it when you saw him last."

"I wasn't ready."

"That's always your excuse."

I swallowed. "Maybe."

"You fell for him."

"I didn't," I protested.

"I can see the sorrow in your eyes."

I shook my head but indeed felt defeated. For billions of years, Satan had fixated on destroying Earth. Then, during the Middle-Ages, he loosened his grip and relaxed. By failing in Japan, I unwittingly ushered in Hell's worst armies. The wars that would ravage the world were some of the darkest in history. And they only got worse.

Beelzebub continued, "No doubt, so could Aaron. That's why you screwed up."

"That's not what happened!"

"Really, so what happened?"

I began pacing, breathed deeply, and finally exclaimed, "Aaron is one of us, isn't he?"

Beelzebub rolled his eyes, pivoted, and started to walk away.

I chased after him and blurted, "Answer me. Is Aaron one of your demons?"

Abruptly, he stopped, glared at me, and laughed. The glimmer in his eyes told me everything. It confirmed my suspicions. Beelzebub had once again set me up.

"I was supposed to be the honeytrap, but

Aaron was the ultimate honeypot." I said to placate Bub.

"Maybe."

"You picked the perfect guy, someone who looked like Jess, Heathcliff, and Prince Genji."

"We know your type, Fina."

"That night at the fashion show. The European who attacked me—he was one of your men?"

Beelzebub's red eyes twinkled. "Perhaps."

"You knew Jess would jump in to save me. Then, you set up a fake email pretending to be Jess, deliberately knowing I'd write novella-length emails."

"You're very predictable and write way too much."

I swallowed. "You knew that I'd feel loss when Jess disappeared."

"Stop it, Fina. No one controls your feelings. No one except you."

I shook my head. "You knew I was vulnerable after the soap casting due to the heating mask Mom gave me. Did you tamper with it?"

"Nope, that's all on your Mom."

"You knew I was down, so you swooped in."

Beelzebub shrugged. "Perfect opportunity."

"You knew if I wore my green dress and beat Aaron at poker, my ego would get inflated, and I'd get carried away. But how did you know this was a personal fantasy?"

"Never a good idea to use your cat's name for

a password."

"So you read my diary?"

Beelzebub laughed like a hyena.

He then mocked my reenactments of Catherine Earnshaw from *Wuthering Heights*: "Heaven did not seem to be my home, and I broke my heart with weeping to come back to Earth, and the angels were so angry that they flung me out into the middle of the heath on the top of Wuthering Heights; where I woke sobbing for joy."

"And you watched my performances from the balcony. You're truly sick, Bub."

"We're all sick, Fina."

I compressed my lips. "I didn't accidentally switch the glasses with the poison? Aaron knew all along."

Beelzebub narrowed his eyes. "If you'd been more focused, that wouldn't have happened."

"Then Aaron appeared –– at the perfect moment, right when the performer attacked me."

"Yes, yes, where are you going with this? I'm bored."

I tilted my head. "Why? Was it because I met with Raphael? The fact that I considered defecting to Heaven?"

"C'mon, Lucifina, you know how it works…"

I took a step backward. "Yes, Hell is all about loyalty."

"Sure."

"Hell didn't want me, but consorting with

your enemies was treason."

"Yes."

With poise and thoughtful reflection, I continued, "But there's more, isn't there?"

Beelzebub arched his eyebrow but said nothing.

"Killing me would have been too easy. That would be merciful."

Beelzebub's mouth tightened. "You're so full of yourself. Do you think anyone gives a damn about an angel?"

"I'm not an angel, and this is about Satan," I stated.

"Finally, you get it."

"Well, I hope you're happy. By shaming me, you've shamed Satan."

My archnemesis sneered. "Goodbye, Lucifina."

I gasped and ran toward him. "Goodbye? You can't leave."

"There's nothing more to say."

"But what about Aaron?" I wanted to confront Bub about what had happened in eleventh-century Japan, but it was best if I didn't. It was to my advantage to let Hell think I'd forgotten the past. Otherwise, they'd know my desire for revenge. It was better to make them think I was a distracted heartsick angel than to let them know my genuine motivations.

Beelzebub paused for a moment and

laughed. "Ha, I should have known."

"What about Aaron?" I repeated.

"Does he even matter, Lucifina? It's like I've said before. You're always pining for some demon in Hell, and it's never about the demon. It's all about Hell."

I continued to do my best to make Bub think I had fallen for Aaron. "Will I see him again?"

Beelzebub spun around while walking backward. With a sly grin, he replied, "Sure, within a thousand years."

I gasped. With a single promise and snide expression, Beelzebub had confirmed my suspicions. My dreams were real. Aaron had betrayed me in one of my former demon lives because I had allowed it. Each succeeding life had sought to redeem the past by deliberately bungling operations to thwart the oppression of Hell. Yet it had never been enough.

Something told me this wasn't over. After all, war is never over. And if I had learned anything in my billions of years as a demon, and even as a professional model, it was that predators always return just when you've forgotten all about them. The question now was who would be the hunter, him or me? Well, now that I remembered myself, it had to be me.

***

Beelzebub vanished.

I remained on the empty terrace, which was

eerily vacant. Had everyone left?

A haunting feeling consumed me.

I ventured to the taxi cue but none were available. I was anxious, so I flew down the marble steps. The clicking of my heels echoed across the driveway and ricocheted through the parking lot.

Alarm gripped me as I feared an attack by anyone lurking in the shadows: a casino patron or a demon. I wandered across the concrete pavement and made my way through the gates and on to the dirt road. My heels were soon soaking in mud.

It was very dark because there were no street lights. So, I kept walking along the side until entering a desolate area filled with shacks and gentle faces in rags. It was a complete contrast to the luxurious casino.

I kept looking and hoping a taxi would appear. None did. On occasion, an angry truck would barrel by and sweep mud on my dress, or a sports car would roar through, causing my hair to blow.

I hopped to avoid stepping into a decaying rat carcass covered in maggots gnawing on bones. I shivered, and my heart quickened because this area was dangerous, but less so than the venue I'd foolishly entered into earlier.

While scurrying as fast as I could to reach the main road, where I might finally find a taxi or a payphone, the sun began to rise. The warm rays cast a glow against my white skin. My spirits immediately lifted. I sighed because I felt incredibly hopeful.

I was free. For years, I'd feared Beelzebub's return. When Hell initially expelled me, there'd been feelings of rejection. Then I romanticized Hell whenever things weren't going well. But in the past three years, I'd been better off on my own.

By allowing Beelzebub to think he'd played me and won, I wouldn't have to worry about Hell seeking revenge for any alleged betrayal.

Demons need to win. It's in their nature. It's best to surrender or let them think they've won. Otherwise, they'll never leave and haunt you for eternity.

Satan wouldn't be impressed by Beelzebub's accomplishments. Nor would anyone else in Hell. They'd all wonder why he'd wasted so much time and energy on a former angel who really wasn't that important.

I was now at an intersection where it was bright. The sun had finished rising, and vendors rushed by with coconut cakes.

I hailed a taxi, hopped in, and headed home.

EPILOGUE

Herman recovered from the blow to his head. He then spent several months at Bangkok Nursing Home's mental care division.

Herman's assault finally broke Dr. Blackie.

Dr. Blackie had long tolerated my family: Khun Jai's loud movements, my absence, and Mom's dogs.

Herman's assault was the final straw for my tuxedoed ally. Dr. Blackie moved out. He spent his last years with our neighbor, Khun Yao, whom he had rescued from choking.

Blackie lived to be twenty, but I never saw him again.

And me? I'm fine. The years after this story were such Hell that I hardly had time to miss the real one.

I remain in exile and am not able to return to the place I once called home.

Freedom of speech is a luxury that only a small portion of the world's population enjoys. That's why many of us write allegories to convey our messages subversively.

If you're confused—well then, I envy the fact that you live in a world so clear and direct you can't imagine the suffering of those who don't possess your freedom.

ABOUT LICIA FLYNN

Licia Flynn grew up attending international schools and obtained a Juris Doctor from a law school in Silicon Valley. Her undergraduate focus was political theory and military history.

On her maternal side, Licia is descended from Irish immigrants who arrived at the Port of New Orleans in the 1800s. Licia's paternal grandparents were educated merchants who fled China in the 1940s.

www.instagram.com/liciaflynn
www.facebook.com/FirmResolveLiciaFlynn
www.twitter.com/FirmResolve
www.klar-marketing.com

FIRM RESOLVE
Licia Flynn

FIRM RESOLVE

LICIA FLYNN

Klar
MC

When an American couple vanishes in Kuala Lumpur, their teenager struggles to survive. Meanwhile, three entrepreneurs envision their Silicon Valley startup. Years later, the company relocates to Shanghai, where its members enjoy a frivolous expat lifestyle. That is until an executive's wife disappears.

Licia Flynn lives in Silicon Valley where she works as a ghostwriter.

ISBN 978-1-7322777-1-7

51795>

Firm Denial, a follow-up to Firm Resolve, is a stand-alone novella.

When a case becomes an obsession, Daniel Petersen leaves Shanghai and hunts down Aaron Walker. The Iraq vet reveals a story that differs significantly from Lana Hayaak's diary entries. Meanwhile, an enigmatic sighting arouses suspicion and threatens national security.

Licia Flynn lives in Silicon Valley where she works as a ghostwriter.

ISBN 978-1-7322777-3-1

51195>

FIRM DENIAL

LICIA FLYNN

Klar MC

FIRM
DENIAL
Licia Flynn